Katie's
new
recipe

SIMON SPOTLIGHT
An imprint of Simon & Schuster Children's Publishing Division
1230 Avenue of the Americas, New York, New York 10020
Copyright © 2013 by Simon & Schuster, Inc.
All rights reserved, including the right of reproduction in whole or in part in any form.
SIMON SPOTLIGHT and colophon are registered
trademarks of Simon & Schuster, Inc.
Text by Tracey West
Chapter header illustrations by Elizabeth Doyle
Designed by Laura Roode
For information about special discounts for bulk purchases, please contact
Simon & Schuster Special Sales
at 1-866-506-1949 or business@simonandschuster.com.
Manufactured in the United States of America 1213 OFF
First Edition 10 9 8 7 6 5 4 3 2
ISBN 978-1-4424-7168-9
ISBN 978-1-4424-7169-6 (eBook)
Library of Congress Catalog Card Number 2013930134

CUPCAKE DIARIES

Katie's new recipe

by coco simon

Simon Spotlight
New York   London   Toronto   Sydney   New Delhi

CHAPTER 1

It's a Cupcake Code Red!

$\mathcal{M}$ ake me a doggy! Make me a doggy!"

I started to sweat as the adorable five-year-old in front of me looked up with pleading eyes. I knelt down and waved a round helium balloon in front of his face.

"It's not the kind of balloon that you can make into animals," I said, using my sweetest voice. "It's just a regular, fun, yellow balloon, to match the cupcakes! See?"

I pointed to the cupcake table across the small yard, where my friends Alexis and Emma were busy placing dozens of yellow and green cupcakes on matching paper plates.

The little boy's lower lip quivered. "But . . . I . . . want . . . a . . . doggy!" Then he began to bawl.

Panicked, I turned to my best friend, Mia, who was filling balloons behind me.

"Mia! We've got a code red!" I cried.

"Katie, what's wrong?" Mia asked.

I pointed to the sobbing boy. "He wants a dog-shape balloon. I don't know what to do."

Mia quickly retrieved a black marker from her bag under a table and took the balloon from my hand. The marker squeaked as she drew a cute doggy face on the balloon, complete with droopy ears and a tongue sticking out. Thank goodness for a friend who can draw!

She handed it to the boy. "How's this?" she asked.

The boy stopped crying. "It's a doggy! Woof! Woof!" Happy again, he ran off.

I let out a sigh. "Mia to the rescue! Thank you. I knew this wasn't going to be easy. Running a party for a bunch of five-year-olds? It's much easier when we bake the cupcakes, serve the cupcakes, and then get out."

A while ago, my friends and I had started a Cupcake Club. We'd turned it into a pretty successful business, baking cupcakes for all kinds of parties and events.

"It's like Alexis said, it's healthy to branch out,"

Mia pointed out. "We're making a lot more money by running the games and activities."

I gazed around the yard. We had worked hard on this cupcake-themed party for a five-year-old girl named Madison. Last night we were up late baking cupcakes in Madison's favorite colors, yellow and green. This morning we got up early (which I never like to do on a Saturday) to set things up. We had a table where the kids could decorate their own cupcakes.

Later, we were going to set up the stuff for the games. We took regular party games and cupcaketized them. You know, instead of Hot Potato, we were going to play Pass the Cupcake. And instead of a donkey, kids could pin a cherry on top of a giant picture of a cupcake. It was going to be fun, but it was definitely a lot of work.

"Well, money isn't everything," I declared. "If Alexis wants us to do this stuff so bad, she can come over here and make balloons. I'm going to go work at the cupcake table. At least I know what I'm doing there."

"Aw, come on, Katie, balloons are fun!" Mia said, bopping me over the head with a green one.

I stuck my tongue out at her. "But crying kids are not! I'll see you later."

I walked across the room to the cupcake-decorating table.

"Alexis, you need to switch with me," I said. "I can't do the balloons. I just don't have it in me."

Alexis nodded, her wavy red hair bouncing on her shoulders. "No problem. There's not much more setting up to do. Mrs. Delfino said that the kids are having pizza in a minute, and then we're going to play some games before we do the cupcake thing."

Alexis walked away, and I took her place behind the table, next to Emma, who really loves dressing up for any event. She wore a light yellow shirt with a short green skirt that matched the cupcakes perfectly. A yellow headband with tiny green flowers held back her straight, blond hair. I had tried to get in the party spirit too, with a yellow T-shirt and green sneakers.

"Katie, you look miserable!" Emma said. "Come on, it's not so bad, is it?"

"I think it's because I'm an only child," I admitted. "I don't know how to deal with little kids."

"That's not true. You're so great with Jake," Emma said. Jake is her six-year-old brother. "He adores you!"

"That's different," I protested. "Jake is only one kid. This is, like, a hundred!"

Emma laughed. "It's only sixteen. But I know what you mean. When Jake's friends are over, it can be too much sometimes."

As we spoke, a woman with curly brown hair stepped into the yard.

"Okay, everybody! It's pizza time! Everyone inside!"

The kids cheered and raced inside, accompanied by the moms who had decided to stay for the party. Alexis approached the cupcake table.

"We should set up the games while everyone eats," she suggested. "Then we'll be ready when they come back out."

"Good idea," Emma agreed. We started to set things up for the games, and after only about ten minutes, the kids came racing back outside.

I shook my head. "Back already? What did they drink with their pizza? Rocket fuel?"

"Games! Games! Games!" the kids started chanting.

Mrs. Delfino smiled at us apologetically. "I hope you don't mind."

"Of course not," Alexis said crisply. When she's on a job, she's all business. "We're ready."

5

"Come on, kids!" Emma said loudly. "Who wants to play Pass the Cupcake?"

Sixteen hands flew into the air at once. "Meeeee!"

I kind of got into it when we played the games. We played Pass the Cupcake first. Mia had sewn a cute cupcake out of felt, and the kids sat in a circle and passed it around when the music played. When the music stopped, the kid holding the cupcake had to leave the circle.

It went pretty well until one little girl started crying when she got out. I almost panicked again. But then I had an idea. I grabbed the girl's hands.

"Everybody outside the circle gets to dance!" I cried, and then I started to dance and twirl around with her. It worked! She stopped crying, and soon all the kids outside the circle were laughing and dancing.

After that, we played Pin the Cherry on the Cupcake using a beautiful poster of a cupcake Mia had drawn, and big cherries cut out of paper. Then we did cupcake relay races, where the runners had to balance a cupcake on the end of a spatula while they were running (instead of the usual egg on a spoon). There was a lot of icing on the grass, but the kids seemed to really like it.

"Great job, everybody!" Alexis called out. "And now it's time to decorate cupcakes. Madison, since you're the birthday girl, you get to go first."

"Yay!" Madison's big brown eyes shone with excitement as she ran to the cupcake table. Her party guests were excited too, and they quickly crowded around her.

"One at a time! One at a time!" Alexis yelled, but the five-year-olds ignored her, swarming around the table and grabbing the cupcakes, sprinkles, and candy toppings.

"Hey! There are spoons for that!" Alexis scolded.

Mia, Emma, and I quickly jumped in to help. I picked up a spoon and tried to show one blond-haired boy how to gently sprinkle some edible green glitter on to his cupcake. He took the spoon from me, dipped it in the glitter . . . and then threw the glitter all over the little girl next to him!

The girl looked stunned. She brushed the green glitter off her face . . . and then started to cry.

"Oh no. Not again," I said, moaning. I didn't think dancing was going to help this one. "We've got another code red!"

But everyone was too busy to come to my rescue. Emma was wiping off frosting from Madison's face, Mia was patiently creating a smiley face made out of candies on another girl's cupcake, and Alexis was marching up and down the table, trying to regain order.

"Icing goes on the cupcake, not on your hands!" she shouted. "And, Leonard, do not put the sprinkle spoon in your mouth!"

Within minutes, the kids were more decorated than the cupcakes.

Mrs. Delfino approached the table, looking flustered. "Oh dear! This is quite a mess!"

We stopped and looked at one another. Our client did not look happy—and that was bad for business.

"It's, um, all part of the fun," I said cheerfully. "And don't worry, we'll clean it up. Who wants to play the Clean-Up Game?"

Sixteen sticky hands flew in the air. "Meeeeeeee!"

Luckily, Emma had thought to pack a big tub of wet wipes. I got out the box and gave one to each kid.

"Okay, now it's time to clean our hands, hands, hands," I instructed in a singsong voice, and luckily, the kids all played along. Next, I had them clean their faces, elbows, and even their knees (that's how messy everyone was!). In the end we had one big pile of messy wet wipes and one yard full of clean kids.

"It's time to sing the birthday song!" Mrs.

Delfino announced, and as the kids followed her inside, we collapsed on the grassy lawn, exhausted.

"Katie, you were so good with the kids!" Mia said.

"Yeah, I'll have to remember that clean-up game for Jake," Emma said.

I frowned. "Well, thanks, but that was still awful. Doesn't this prove we should stick to just cupcakes from now on?"

"Absolutely not," Alexis said. "It just means we need to perfect our plan. Until that big cupcake mess, everything was going really well."

"Yeah." Mia nodded in agreement. "It was kind of fun, too."

"Definitely," said Emma. "And let's not forget the extra money. It's worth it."

I sighed. "I guess you're right. You know me. I don't really like changing the way I do things. In fifth grade, I wore the same pair of purple sneakers every day for a year. My mother said she had to peel them off my feet, literally."

Everyone laughed.

"Don't worry, Katie," Alexis said. "Our new business plan is going to be great. You'll see."

"Fine," I said. "But next time, let's leave the icing *on* the cupcakes, okay?"

9

CHAPTER 2

What's Up with Mom?

I was so tired from the party that I did not want to get out of bed the next morning.

"Katie, it's time to get up!" my mom urged.

I groaned and pulled my pillow over my face. Mom gently tugged the pillow out of my grasp. I opened my eyes to see her brown eyes staring at me through her eyeglasses.

"You know, for years you would wake up at five thirty every morning, no matter what, and come wake *me* up," Mom said. "And now I can't get you out of bed."

"So . . . tired . . . ," I said dramatically.

"Well, I made pancakes," Mom said. "So please come down and eat them before they get cold."

I quickly sat up. "Blueberry?"

Mom smiled. "Of course," she replied, and then she left my room. That got me up. Mom's pancakes are the best, even if she sometimes still makes them with little smiley faces with the blueberries. It's like she forgets that I'm in middle school now.

A few minutes later I was sitting at the kitchen table, eating pancakes with my mom.

"So I didn't get the details about the party yesterday," she said. "How did it go?"

"It was a mess!" I said, and then I told her everything that happened.

Mom laughed. "Well, it sounds like it worked out all right in the end."

"I guess," I said. "But I hope we don't do too many more parties like that. It's a lot of work!"

"A little hard work never hurt anyone," Mom said, and I shook my head.

"You sound like Grandpa Chuck," I said.

"Speaking of work, what's your homework situation?" Mom asked.

I had to think. "Um, one math worksheet and an essay for English," I reported. "I'll do it right after breakfast."

"Do you mind if I go for a run, then?" Mom asked. "I mean, unless you want me to wait for you."

"Go ahead," I said with a yawn. "I'm too tired to run today, anyway."

Mom smiled and then started to clean up the breakfast dishes. She started to sing a song while she worked.

"Mom, it's my turn to do those," I said. "I just want to sit here for a few minutes first."

"Oh, don't worry about it," Mom said cheerfully. "I don't mind."

Then she started singing again.

Wow, Mom's in a good mood today, I thought.

After breakfast I showered, put on a tie-dyed T-shirt, and jeans, and then settled down at the clean kitchen table to get my homework done. If I don't start it in the morning, then Mom starts asking what the "plan" is for the day. She gets kind of mad when I leave it all for Sunday night. I was halfway through my math worksheet when Mom came into the kitchen.

"I'll be back in about an hour," she said.

"I'm already doing my math worksheet," I said, holding up my paper. That's when I noticed Mom's outfit.

Normally, Mom wears her favorite sweatpants when we go running, the blue ones with the big white streak across the front from that time she accidentally got bleach on them. She pairs them with any old T-shirt and doesn't care if it matches. And she pulls her curly hair back into a ponytail. Sometimes, in the winter, she even runs in her pajamas.

But today she had on a pair of black running pants that looked brand new, and instead of an old T-shirt, she had on a pretty lavender top I hadn't seen before, with flowers stitched around the neckline. She wore a matching light purple headband in her hair, and she even had on lip gloss. And it wasn't clear—it was pink!

"Mom, why are you so dressed up to go running?" I asked. "You usually only ever wear lip gloss when we go out to a fancy restaurant or something."

Then I also noticed that she wasn't wearing her glasses, either! "And why do you have your contacts in? You always complain about your contact lenses and try to wear them as little as possible. You *never* run with your contacts."

Mom blushed. "It's no big deal," she said. "It's kind of a New Year's resolution to spruce myself up a little bit."

"But New Year's was months ago," I pointed out.

"Well, a belated one," Mom said. "Mia's mom is

such a fashion plate. I didn't want you to feel like you have the slacker mom."

"I've never felt that way!" I insisted. "Besides, I'm your slacker daughter. We match."

When I said it out loud, I realized that I like how Mom and I are alike in some ways, besides the fact we both have brown hair and brown eyes. My dad left my mom and me when I was just a baby, so it's just been the two of us for my whole life. We're like a team.

Mom laughed at my slacker comment. "Well, it makes me feel good to dress up a little," she said.

"Suit yourself," I told her. "But I am telling you I am *not* wearing lip gloss the next time we go running. You are on your own with that stuff."

"I don't expect you to," Mom said. She leaned over and kissed my forehead. "Be back soon."

I shook my head as she left. Parents can be so weird sometimes! But if it meant I got pancakes and Mom did the dishes, then whatever was going on was okay with me.

CHAPTER 3

Middle School Spirit!

So, this year of middle school has been a lot easier in some ways. I know my way around now, and I'm used to changing to a different teacher for every class. I have also mastered the art of opening up a combination lock, which isn't as easy as it looks.

In other ways, it's been a little bit harder. Like, when the school year started, Mia made friends with this new girl, Olivia, and I thought she was going to replace me as Mia's best friend. That wasn't fun. But Olivia ended up being friends with the girls in the Best Friends Club instead, so everything worked out okay. Besides, I know that even if Mia makes new friends, she will always be my friend too.

Another hard thing—well, not hard, really,

maybe more like strange—is my friendship with George Martinez. We've known each other since kindergarten, and I think he's really funny. But a while ago we started liking each other. You know, like, *liking* each other. He asked me to dance at the fall dance, and we went to the pep-rally parade together. And that was nice and everything, but now when we're in a normal situation, like riding the school bus, it's kind of awkward. I don't know what to say or do around him.

I guess that's one example of how I don't like when things change. Before George and I *liked* each other, everything was simple. But now it's kind of complicated.

Anyway, I don't have to worry about George or Olivia at lunch, because George sits with his friends, Olivia sits with the BFC, and I sit with the Cupcake Club. On Wednesday, the Cupcake Club and I were talking about the big announcement we'd heard in homeroom that morning.

"I can't believe it's only a few weeks until Spirit Day," Alexis complained. "Ugh!"

"I thought the last one was fun," Mia said.

"That's because you were on a team with cool people," Alexis pointed out. "I got stuck with Sydney, remember?"

Sydney Whitman used to be the leader of the BFC (except they used to be called the Popular Girls Club), and she wasn't always very nice. Thankfully, she moved away during the summer.

"I kind of agree with Alexis," I said. "I know those games we play are supposed to get us to bond or whatever. But competition makes me anxious. It's too much pressure to have fun!"

"I like it, just as long as I don't have to do the egg race," Emma said with a shudder.

"What's wrong with the egg race?" Mia asked.

"Trust us, don't ask," Alexis said. She and Emma had gone to a different elementary school than I did (and Mia grew up in Manhattan). They knew a lot about each other that Mia and I still didn't know, even though it felt like we'd all been friends forever.

Emma sighed. "Well, maybe we'll be on the same team."

Alexis shook her head. "I swear, they know who we're all friends with, and they break us up on purpose."

I nodded. "Exactly. Bonding, just like I said."

"Well, it's ridiculous," Alexis retorted. "You can't force people to bond."

"Look on the bright side," I said. "At least we don't have to go to class."

Alexis just looked at me. "Seriously?"

That was the wrong thing to say to Alexis. She likes school. And so do I, really, but it's nice to take a break from writing essays and solving math problems sometimes.

By the time Mia and I rode the bus home from school, the conversation had moved on from the topic of Spirit Day. Instead, we were talking about our upcoming social studies test.

"I don't know how I feel about the industrial revolution," I said. "I mean, I think it was kind of nice back when everyone made most things by hand."

"But way harder," Mia remarked. "I mean, I like to sew, but if I had to sew all my own clothes, I'd never get anything else done!"

George popped up from the seat behind us. "I agree with Katie," he volunteered. "Factories make too much pollution. It might be easier, but it's destroying the planet."

Secretly, I was pleased that George agreed with me. But I responded by teasing him.

"Hey, you shouldn't be eavesdropping," I said.

"Why? Are you talking about something personal?" He waggled his eyebrows.

"Like we would do that on a school bus," Mia said, rolling her eyes. "We don't talk about anything personal."

"Personal?" asked George. "Like, what do you talk about that's personal?"

"It's personal, George!" cried Mia. "That means you don't talk about it."

"Do you talk about me?" he asked with a smile.

I blushed and Mia rolled her eyes again.

Remember what I said before? Now the conversation was getting weird. Luckily, the bus pulled up at my stop.

"See you tomorrow!" I said with a wave, and got off fast.

My house is only a couple of blocks from the bus stop. Wednesdays are my mom's day off, so she's usually home when I get there. But when I turned the corner, I didn't see her car. I used my key to get inside.

"Mom?" I called, but there was no answer.

On the kitchen table was a plate of Mom's homemade oatmeal-raisin cookies and a note.

I'll be back in time for dinner. Please text me when you get home. Love you! Mom

I didn't think too much about it. To be honest, this was the first year Mom let me stay home when she went out, and I kind of like it. It means I'm not some little kid anymore. I always text her and she checks in on me, but that's okay.

Home! Thanks for the cookies! I texted.
Enjoy them! Mom texted back.

She usually tells me to start my homework, but she didn't this time.

I ate the cookies and did my homework. I was watching some videos on my laptop when I heard the front door open.

"Hello!" Mom called out.

"Hi!" I called back, my eyes glued to the computer screen.

Mom walked into the kitchen. "Hello," she said again.

I looked up and couldn't believe my eyes. Mom's curly hair was straight and cut into a bob with long bangs! She carried two big shopping bags from Carrie and Company, this store in the mall that a lot of moms shop at.

"Whoa!" I exclaimed.

Mom put down the bags and pointed to her

new hair. "Well, Katie, what do you think?"

"It's nice," I said honestly. "But it's . . . really different. You don't look like you anymore."

Mom laughed. "Well, I'm still me."

I nodded to the bags. "What's all that?"

"I went shopping with Sara," she said. "She helped me pick out some new outfits."

"You went shopping with Mia's mom?" I asked in disbelief. Mia's mom is a shopping kind of mom. My mom has never been a shopping kind of mom. She'll wear the same stuff over and over until it wears out.

"I'm lucky I know a professional stylist," Mom said. "She helped me find the most amazing dress. I can't wait to show you!"

My eyes narrowed. "Are you craving garlic by any chance?" I asked.

Mom looked confused. "No? Why?"

"Because I saw this old movie once where these aliens invade Earth and take over people, and the only way you can tell who's an alien and who isn't is that the aliens love to eat garlic," I explained. "I need to make sure you're not an alien. Because you are definitely not acting like the real Sharon Brown."

"Very funny," Mom said drily. "I'm going to try

on my new dress. Why don't you order us a pizza?"

I looked at her for a second. We usually had pizza on Saturday nights as a treat. Mom is pretty strict about eating healthy foods, and even though we get veggies on our pizza, she still won't count it as a "healthy" dinner. But pizza during the week was . . . unusual. Still, I didn't want to point that out.

"Sure. What do you want on it?" I asked.

Mom grinned. "Extra garlic!"

"*Not* funny," I shot back at her.

When I picked up my phone, I didn't call the pizzeria right away. Instead, I texted Mia.

Katie: Something is wrong with my mom! She's got a haircut and now she's shopping with ur mom! What is wrong with her?

Mia: LOL! Nothing. Sometimes people like 2 change things up. When my mom got divorced she got a whole new wardrobe. It was still black, but all new.

Katie: My mom got divorced ages ago. This is just weird.

Mia: Don't worry. She'll get over it.

Katie: I hope so.

But I had a strange feeling that whatever was going on with Mom was just the beginning.

CHAPTER 4

I Spy

The rest of the week I made a special effort to keep an eye on Mom, and I noticed a bunch of things. She wore lip gloss every single day. She got up extra early to specially blow-dry her hair, so it would stay straight the whole day. She sang all the time to herself, under her breath. And at night, when I was in my room, I could hear her in her room, talking on the phone and laughing a lot.

Maybe she's talking to Grandma Carole, I told myself, but I didn't quite believe it. I knew her I'm-on-the-phone-with–Grandma-Carole laugh. This laugh was higher, and it lasted longer.

The whole thing was distracting.

On Fridays the Cupcake Club always meets during lunch. Today, Alexis was telling us we had booked a big job with the school PTA, but I was barely listening.

"So we'll meet next week at Mia's house," Alexis said. "Is that okay for everybody?"

Mia nodded, and Emma said, "Sure," but I didn't answer. I absently took a bite out of one of the strawberries-and-cream cupcakes that Emma had baked for Cupcake Friday.

"Katie? Next Saturday at Mia's?" Alexis repeated.

"Oh, sorry, sure," I replied.

"Are you okay, Katie?" Mia asked. "You're superquiet."

"I'm just thinking about my mom, that's all," I said.

Emma looked alarmed. "Oh no! Is she all right?"

"She went shopping with my mom the other day," Mia explained. "And she got a new haircut, and Katie's freaking out about it."

"It's not just that," I said defensively. "She's been acting, like, weird and stuff."

"People get their hair cut all the time," Alexis said.

"Yeah, but this was, like, way different," I said. It was hard to explain, and suddenly, I didn't feel like talking about it. "Never mind."

Alexis shrugged. "So, anyway, we're on for a

meeting next Saturday. And movie night at my house tonight, right?"

"I'll be at my dad's," said Mia. Because her parents are divorced, she spends every other weekend in Manhattan with him. I guess I'd be doing that if my dad lived close by, but Mom told me he moved to Washington or something. Anyway, he doesn't even call me anymore, so it doesn't matter.

Emma hugged Mia. "You'll be there in spirit! But we'll still miss you."

"It's okay," Mia said. "Dad and I go out for sushi on Fridays, and I am really in the mood for some spicy tuna."

So, that night after dinner, Mom got ready to drop me off at Alexis's house. She was all dressed up in a black dress and heels, and her hair was supershiny and straight.

"Are you going somewhere?" I asked her.

Mom blushed a little. "Just out with some friends. From the office."

"Okay." Why shouldn't she go out with some friends? She was allowed to get dressed up if she wanted to. I started to feel silly. Mia was probably right—Mom was just trying out a new look. But then I started wondering which friends she was going out with. Her partner was Dr. White, and he was really old. It would be hard to believe he was going out on a Friday night.

When we got to Alexis's house, Mom got out of the car.

"I need to go in and talk to Mrs. Becker for a minute," she said. "She said she had a question for me about dental implants."

Did I mention that my mom is a dentist? Everyone is always asking her about their teeth.

Alexis answered when we rang the bell, and she raised her eyebrows when she saw my mom.

"Oh, hi, Mrs. Brown," she said. Then she almost did a double take. "Wow, you look really nice."

"Thank you, Alexis," my mom said. "Is your mother around?"

Alexis nodded to the kitchen. "Sure. Come in."

I followed my mom inside, and Alexis dragged me into the living room.

"Oh my gosh! I see what you mean about your mom. Is she going out on a date?" Alexis asked.

I was pretty shocked. "A date? No! No way. I mean, my mom doesn't date."

Now Alexis looked surprised. "But she's been single for years, right? It makes sense that she would date."

Honestly, I had never thought about my mom dating anyone. I mean, she was my *mom*.

"Well, she's just going out with some friends from the office," I said.

"Okay," Alexis replied, and shrugged her shoulders as if to say *Whatever*, but by the tone of her voice, I could tell that she didn't believe it.

By the end of the night, I wasn't sure if I believed it, either. When Mom picked me up, she was extra happy and smiley.

"So, did you have a good time with your *friends*?" I asked, emphasizing the last word.

"Wonderful!" Mom answered. If she noticed what I was hinting at, she didn't let on.

Then the next morning Mom knocked on my door at seven thirty.

"I'm going for a run!" she said. "Be back soon!"

I sat up, rubbing my eyes. She didn't even ask me if I wanted to go with her! Sure, it was way too early for running. But that didn't matter. It was the principle of the thing.

I bolted out of bed. I was about to do something kind of wrong, but I felt like I couldn't stop myself. I quickly got dressed in sweats, a T-shirt, and sneakers.

I was going to spy on my mom. It was the only way I was going to find out the truth.

I waited until I heard the front door close. Then I ran downstairs and peeked out the front door. I waited until Mom jogged around the corner, and then I left the house.

Following her was pretty easy, because it looked like she was taking our usual route to the park. I stayed a block behind her the whole way.

When I reached the park, I knew I had to be careful. I ran behind a tree and looked out, hoping to see which path she was taking. I kind of felt like I was in one of those spy movies.

Mom got to the start of the path that goes around the pond—and then she stopped in front of a guy wearing blue sweats. He looked really happy to see her—and then he kissed her on the cheek!

Then he said something, and Mom laughed, flipping her hair behind her neck. It almost looked like she was . . . flirting!

Suddenly, I felt awful, like I was seeing something I wasn't supposed to see. I never should have spied on my mom. It was a dumb thing to do.

I quickly turned and ran back home. But with each step, I stopped feeling guilty and grew more and more angry. Was Mom dating that guy? And if she was, why was she keeping it a secret?

Wait until she gets home, I thought. But then I realized if I confronted Mom, I'd have to admit that I was spying on her, and she wouldn't like that one bit.

Frustrated, I ran up to my room, kicked off my sneakers, and crawled back under the covers. I wished I could start the day all over again!

CHAPTER 5

Sleepover Drama

Things were kind of strained between me and Mom after that. I didn't really talk to her a lot. The funny thing is, Mom didn't even seem to notice. She kept singing and humming and fixing her hair and applying lip gloss like everything was normal—but it wasn't!

I didn't tell Mia or any of my other friends about the guy I saw with Mom in the park. I'm not exactly sure why I kept it a secret. Mostly, I didn't feel like talking about it, and I hated that Alexis might be right about Mom dating. But part of me also hoped that maybe if I ignored the whole thing, it would just go away.

That Friday night, I thought I might be right. When Mom got home from work, she changed into jeans and a normal shirt. Then she came down into the kitchen.

"I was thinking of making some chicken tacos tonight," she said. "Want to help?"

"Sure," I replied, and the rest of the night was a pretty normal night with Mom. We made dinner, and then we played board games, and then we jogged to the ice-cream place that just opened for the season and got ice-cream cones. I always get mine with rainbow sprinkles.

The next night, the Cupcake Club was having a sleepover at Mia's so that we could plan for the PTA dinner. Mom dropped me off at Mia's at four o'clock, and she was still wearing her jeans and sneakers.

"Tomorrow I'll pick you up around ten, so we can go running," Mom said.

"Okay," I said, grinning. "Try not to miss me too much."

Mom smiled. "Don't worry. I've got a good book to read."

She gave me a kiss, and I headed into Mia's house. When Mia opened the door, her two little fluffy white dogs ran up to me, yipping and sniffing my shoes.

"Hi, Tiki! Hi, Milkshake!" I said, leaning down

to pet them. Once they were satisfied, they quickly scampered away.

"You can put your stuff in my room," Mia said. "Come on!"

I followed her upstairs. "It's awfully quiet. Where's Dan?" Dan was Mia's stepbrother, and usually you can hear heavy metal music blasting from his room.

"He said he didn't want to be in a house with so many girls in it tonight, so he's sleeping at his friend's house," Mia explained. "I don't know what he's worried about. We're not so bad."

She pushed open her bedroom door, and I dropped my overnight bag and sleeping bag on the fluffy white carpet. Mia's room is pretty amazing; the walls are pale turquoise, and she and her stepdad painted the furniture white with black trim. It looks like a fancy fashion boutique or something (whereas my room, on the other hand, is basically a colorful but comfortable mess).

Then the doorbell rang, and we ran downstairs to greet Alexis and Emma. Mia's mom and her stepdad, Eddie, came out of the kitchen to say hello.

"Wow, look at all of you!" Eddie joked. "I'm outnumbered. Maybe Dan had the right idea."

I think Eddie is pretty nice. Mia is lucky to have a stepdad like him. I suddenly thought of that guy in the park. Was he my future stepdad? And would he be nice, like Eddie, or mean?

Eddie gently punched my arm. "Hey, kiddo, I'm making your favorite tonight. Vegetable lasagna!"

"Oh, great! Thanks, Mr. Valdes," I said. But I wasn't exactly feeling hungry.

"Don't forget, we need the kitchen later," Mia said. "We're going to do a test batch of cupcakes for the PTA dinner."

Alexis held up a shopping bag. "We've been talking about trying to do chocolate marshmallow cupcakes for a while, so I picked up some ingredients. We might want to make them for a client sometime."

"You can put them right into the kitchen, Alexis," said Mia's mom. "Mia, please bring your friends' bags upstairs."

Soon we were all in Mia's room, hanging out. Sometimes when the Cupcake Club gets together, we are all business, making plans and thinking up recipes. But other times we just do normal stuff. Mia wanted to show us this video for a new song, and soon we were dancing around the room like crazy.

"Isn't this the best song ever?" Mia shouted over the music.

"I like it!" Alexis agreed. She was shaking her head back and forth, and her red hair looked like a cloud around her face.

I started copying Alexis, and it felt pretty good. My weird mood was gone, just like that, and I was glad.

Then we had Eddie's vegetable lasagna, which was delicious, and lots of salad and garlic bread. After dinner we helped clean up the kitchen and then got to work on our chocolate marshmallow cupcakes.

I'm usually the one who comes up with the recipes, and so I had brought some baking tools with me.

"There's a few ways to do a chocolate marshmallow cupcake," I said as we sat around the kitchen table. "We could do a chocolate cupcake with marshmallow icing. Or put marshmallow fluff inside a chocolate cupcake. Or, we could stir mini marshmallows into a chocolate cupcake. I think we can use our basic chocolate recipe for all of those."

"Mmm, they all sound good," said Emma.

Alexis started unpacking the bag of ingredients

she brought. "I got regular marshmallows, tiny marshmallows, and marshmallow fluff, just in case," she said. "Let's make batter for two dozen cupcakes."

We got to work on the batter first. We've made so many cupcakes that we can do it pretty quickly now. Cream the butter and sugar, add the eggs and vanilla, mix the dry ingredients, add the dry to the wet, and bam! Cupcakes.

"If they ever had a speed cupcake-making competition, we'd rule," I said as I used an ice-cream scoop to put the perfect amount of batter in each baking tin's cup.

"Definitely," Mia agreed.

Mia's mom had preheated the oven for us, and she supervised as we carefully slid the pans inside. Then we got to work on the toppings.

"Okay," Alexis said. "Eight of the cupcakes will get marshmallow icing. Do we have a recipe for that?"

I nodded. "It's almost like a buttercream frosting, but you use marshmallow fluff."

"Check," Alexis said. "So what about the other two? One will have marshmallow fluff inside, and the other has little marshmallows in it."

"We could put the marshmallow frosting on

those too," Mia suggested. "Like a double blast of marshmallow."

"Or chocolate frosting," Emma said thoughtfully.

"So let's make a batch of those too," Alexis suggested.

We had the frostings done by the time the cupcakes came out of the oven. We had to put them in the refrigerator to cool so the icing wouldn't melt when we applied it. When they were cool, I took four cupcakes and used my cupcake plunger to punch a small hole into the middle of each one.

"Katie and her cupcake tools," Mia said with a smile. "That is so awesome!"

"I love it," I admitted. "And now we just fill the hole with the marshmallow fluff, see?"

I used a small spoon to fill the hole.

"It's a little messy," I said, "but when we frost it, it won't matter."

Soon we had a platter of cupcakes done a bunch of different ways.

"Taste-test time!" Emma announced.

"I'd better get Eddie," Mia said. "He won't want to miss this."

Mia left the kitchen and came back with her mom and stepdad. We cut the cupcakes into fourths, so we could taste each version without experiencing cupcake overload. Alexis took careful notes as we gave our feedback.

"So, most of us felt the mini marshmallows melted too much inside the batter," she said. "Plain chocolate with marshmallow frosting was good, but plain chocolate with marshmallow filling and marshmallow icing was the best."

"But a little sticky," Mrs. Valdes remarked.

Mia picked up the winning cupcake. "And it's a little plain, too. We'd have to come up with some awesome decorations for it."

"You're great at that," I told Mia.

"Thanks," she said. "But normally we have a theme. Do we have a theme for the PTA dinner?"

Alexis frowned. "I totally forgot about that. We need to do some brainstorming."

Mia's mom glanced at the clock. "Girls, it's already past ten, and you still need to clean the kitchen. Maybe that could wait until the morning."

"Sounds good to me," Alexis said.

"I should call my mom," I said. "She said she was going to pick me up kind of early. I'll see if I can stay later."

I washed my hands and dialed Mom at home on

my cell phone. The phone at our house rang and rang and then went to voice mail.

"Mom? It's Katie. Are you there?" And then I realized that of course she couldn't hear me.

"That's really weird," I remarked. "Mom didn't answer."

"Maybe she's asleep," Alexis suggested.

"She always stays up late on Saturdays," I said. "Let me try her cell."

I dialed the number, and she picked up after one ring. "Katie? Is everything okay?" She sounded panicked. Mom is such a worrywart.

"I just needed to ask you something," I said.

"Well, it's just so late," Mom said. "Usually when someone calls this late, it's an emergency."

That's when I noticed the noise in the background.

"Mom, are you home?" I asked.

There was a pause. "Oh, I'm out with a friend for dinner," she said.

A friend? "I thought you were reading a book," I said.

"Well, I was, but my plans changed," Mom said. "Katie, I'm the mom here, remember? There's no need to grill me. What's your question?"

"I just wanted to know if you can pick me up a

little later tomorrow morning," I said. "Like, maybe I can call you when we're done figuring out this cupcake stuff."

"Of course!" Mom replied. "Have fun, okay? I love you."

"Love you too." I ended the call, then said, "That was weird."

"So when she doesn't answer, it's weird, and when she answers, it's weird too?" Alexis asked.

I sighed. "Never mind."

So Mom was out with a friend. Was it that friend from the park? I didn't want to think about it.

"Come on," I said, picking up a sponge. "Let's clean up."

CHAPTER 6

A Cupcake Alliance

*H*ave you ever had a sleepover where you stay up all night? Well, we tried to do that, but we were all so tired from making cupcakes that we fell asleep before midnight.

Mia's mom woke us up around nine.

"Breakfast is ready," she said. "I know you girls are sleepy, but it sounds like you still have some work to do."

I sat up and yawned. "I am sooooooo sleepy!"

Alexis yawned too. "Me too. But Mia's mom is right."

About a half hour later, fortified by bacon and eggs, we all sat around Mia's dining room table, brainstorming.

"So we need a theme for our PTA cupcakes,"

Alexis began. "PTA is 'Parent Teacher Association.' Like an alliance."

"Like the Rebel Alliance in *Star Wars*?" I asked, and Emma giggled.

"*Star Wars* cupcakes would be fun, but not for this," Alexis said. "What's another word for an alliance? Like, joining forces?"

"Exactly. May the force be with you," I said, and everyone laughed.

"How about . . . things that go together," Mia suggested.

Alexis nodded. "I love it! Classic pairings."

"Like R2-D2 and C-3PO?" I joked. I couldn't help it.

"More like chocolate and vanilla," Mia said. "Strawberries and cream."

"Sugar and spice!" Emma added.

"Or peanut butter and jelly," I said, deciding to be serious.

Alexis was writing down everything. "These are all good ideas for cupcake combinations. We just have to find the right one."

"You can't go wrong with chocolate and vanilla," Mia said. "Everyone loves that. And maybe we could ice half of a cupcake in vanilla and half in chocolate. Like a black-and-white cookie."

"Then what flavor would the cupcake be?" Emma asked.

"We could do a chocolate-and-vanilla swirl," I said. "They're kind of a pain to do, but it would be cool."

"We should do a test batch," Alexis said.

I groaned. I love baking cupcakes, but I was starting to feel cupcaked-out.

"Just one batch," Alexis said. "We're running out of time to get this right. The PTA president is expecting a proposal and sample in two weeks."

"Let's do it," I said. "We'll need two batches each of batter and frosting."

We got to work, and about an hour and a half later we had a dozen chocolate-and-vanilla cupcakes in front of us. Eddie walked into the kitchen, and his eyes got wide.

"More cupcakes! I'm going to need to go on a diet." He rubbed his belly.

"After you taste this," Mia said, handing him one.

"If you insist," Eddie said with a grin. He took a bite, and we all waited for his reaction. "Mmm. Delicious as always."

"But did you get the whole chocolate-and-vanilla thing?" Alexis asked.

"In the frosting, definitely," he replied. "But maybe not so much in the cupcake part."

We each tried half a cupcake, and Eddie was right. The swirl looked pretty, but it tasted mostly like a chocolate cupcake, not a mix of both.

Alexis sighed and put down the cupcake. "Back to the drawing board. What about Katie's peanut-butter-and-jelly idea? It's a classic pairing. And it kind of goes with a school theme, because a lot of kids eat it for lunch."

"And a P-B-and-J cupcake is what started our whole Cupcake Club," Emma pointed out.

That was true. The very first day I met Mia, Emma, and Alexis, my mom had made me a P-B-and-J cupcake. It's part of how we became friends.

"I love it," Mia said. "But it might not be sophisticated enough for an adult crowd, you know? Maybe we can spice it up somehow."

"Ooh, I get it!" Emma said excitedly. "Like maybe the peanut-butter frosting could have a kick of ginger."

"Or maybe instead of grape jam, we could use raspberry or something," Alexis suggested.

Emma nodded. "I like that. We could go really exotic with the jam, like . . . I don't know . . .

maybe apricot. Or gooseberry. They have those at the gourmet food shop in town."

"Hold on for a second," I said. "I thought we wanted to do a classic pairing. Peanut butter and grape jelly is classic. We shouldn't mess with a good thing."

"We should do some more test batches," Alexis suggested. "Then we can vote on the best."

"But not today," Emma said. "I've got to get home soon. I'm on Jake duty this afternoon."

"Then let's figure out a time in the next week," Alexis said.

We checked our schedules and figured out that Friday would be best. I offered to do it at my house. Then we cleaned up, and Emma headed home. Alexis called her dad and I called my mom for a ride home. Mr. Becker got to Mia's house first, so Mia and I were alone for a little bit.

"So, are you and your mom going clothes shopping today?" Mia teased. "I know how much you love that."

"*Not,*" I replied. "I think we'll probably go for a run together. Unless . . ."

"Unless what?" Mia asked.

I thought about telling Mia about the guy I saw with mom in the park. But I still didn't feel like talking about it. Then Mia's mom came into the living room.

"Mia, Eddie and I need to go to the carpet store. Do you want to come with us?" she asked.

"No, that's okay," Mia said.

Mrs. Valdes walked away.

"So, do your mom and Eddie do stuff together a lot?" I asked casually.

Mia shrugged. "I guess. They're married, so they're supposed to, right?"

I didn't answer her, because I didn't know. It had just been Mom and me for my whole life. I was used to having her around. What if she was serious about this park guy? I'd have to share her.

A car horn beeped outside.

"Your mom's here," Mia said.

"Yeah," I said. To myself I thought, *But for how long?*

CHAPTER 7

The Challenge

Mom was in a really good mood when she picked me up. When we got home she made a big pot of chicken soup for dinner, and she was singing the whole time she chopped the vegetables—even the onions, and I know she hates doing that!

After dinner I was in kind of a mellow mood, so I got comfortable on the couch and started flipping through the channels. That's when I saw that the last *Harry Potter* movie was coming on at nine o'clock. I've seen it, like, three times already, but I was totally in a mood to see it again. Then I noticed it wasn't over until eleven, which is past my bedtime on a school night.

Since Mom was in such a good mood, though, I thought I'd ask her.

"Hey, Mom," I said, poking my head through her bedroom doorway. "Can I stay up until a little after eleven to watch the last *Harry Potter* movie?"

Mom was humming and hanging up clothes in her closet. "Sure, Katie," she said. "Have fun!"

I hurried back into the living room before she could change her mind. If sneaking around behind my back was going to put her in a good mood, I might as well take advantage of it, right?

So that's what I did for the next few days. On Monday, I hinted that it might be nice to get ice cream again, and fifteen minutes later I was eating a delicious cone with rainbow sprinkles. On Tuesday, I got to stay up an extra half hour to watch the results show of *Teen Singing Stars*. On Wednesday, I made a marshmallow-fluff-and-peanut-butter sandwich for myself for lunch, and Mom didn't say a thing. (Normally she would freak out, and I'd get a nutrition lecture.) Thursday, I convinced her to take me to the bookstore, so I could get the latest book in the Emerald Forest series, which I love.

Did I feel guilty, taking advantage of Mom's good mood like that? Well, maybe just a tiny bit. But not enough to stop doing it.

Friday was awesome because Mia, Emma, and Alexis came over for a cupcake meeting. Mom and

I bought peanut butter and grape jelly for the test batch of our classic P-B-and-J cupcakes, and Emma came with a little bag full of fancy jellies.

"We can try them all and see which one we like best," Emma said. "Then we can finally settle this jam jam."

"Or is it a jelly jam?" I joked.

"Either way, we're in a jam," Alexis said. "So let's get jamming!"

To better taste the flavors of jelly, we baked a batch of vanilla cupcakes and whipped up a bowl of peanut-butter frosting, using the same recipes we always used. Then I used my cupcake plunger to punch a hole in each one, just like I had done with the marshmallow cupcakes. Emma carefully filled three cupcakes with grape jelly, three cupcakes with apricot jelly, three with raspberry jelly, and three with guava jelly. Then we covered each cupcake with the peanut-butter frosting.

I sniffed the guava jelly in the jar. "I've never had this before. What is it?"

"It's a tropical fruit," Emma explained. "I'm not sure what it tastes like. I've never had it before, either, but I thought it looked interesting."

We sliced the cupcakes, so we could have a little taste of each batch. I didn't like the apricot with the peanut butter at all. The guava was interesting; kind of like a cross between a strawberry and a pear. Not too sweet. The raspberry was just okay, but I definitely liked the grape the best.

"I vote for grape," I said, speaking up first.

"I don't know, Katie," Emma said. "The grape is good, but I really like the guava."

Mia nodded. "It definitely has that sophisticated flavor we were looking for."

"It's good for business to use unusual ingredients," Alexis joined in. "It sets us apart from other cupcake bakers."

"But grape is classic," I protested. "I thought we wanted classic."

"Well, three of us want guava, so you're outvoted," Alexis said. "Majority rules."

For some reason, this made me really upset.

"So that's how it's going to be? Three against one?" I asked, and I could feel my cheeks getting hot.

"Well, a vote is a fair way to do it," Alexis said. "But if you're upset . . ."

Emma looked at me with those sympathetic blue eyes of hers. "It's nothing against you, Katie. It's just nice to try something new sometimes."

I sighed and looked down at my sneakers. I

suddenly felt really sad. "Maybe I don't want to try something new. Maybe I want things to stay the same."

Then Mia tried to smooth things over, and she knew just what to say—she always does.

"How about this?" she began. "If you try baking the guava cupcakes, I'll try something new too."

I have to admit, I was intrigued. "Like what?" I asked.

"Well, I haven't thought it through yet," Mia replied. "But I'll think of something."

"What if you wore a sweatshirt and jeans to school?" Alexis suggested.

Mia turned pale at the idea. I swear, she looked like she was going to faint.

"A . . . *sweat*shirt?" she repeated, mortified. "Does it have to be something so major? I mean, Katie just needs to agree to a cupcake flavor."

You might not know this about Mia, but she's totally into fashion. She doesn't mind dressing down sometimes, but she absolutely, positively hates sweatshirts. I knew this would be a hard thing for her to do.

I couldn't help it. I started to laugh. "Oh my gosh, I would love to see that! Come on, Mia, how bad could it be?"

"When I wear a sweatshirt, I feel like a . . . like a giant potato sack or something," Mia protested. "They're awful!"

"They're soft and warm and cozy," I countered. "Besides, it's only for a day."

Mia sighed. "Fine. I'll do it. But then Alexis and Emma should do something too."

Now Alexis looked a little panicked. "Like what?"

"You were pretty good at thinking up something for me," Mia pointed out.

"I think I know something for Emma," I said, remembering a recent conversation we all had. "She could do the egg race on Spirit Day."

Now Emma turned pale. "Not the egg race!"

"What exactly happened at that egg race, anyway?" Mia asked.

Emma looked at Alexis. "You tell it. It's too painful for me to repeat."

Alexis shrugged. "It's not that complicated. We were doing the egg race when we were in fourth grade—"

"Third grade," Emma corrected.

"Okay, third grade. Emma was carrying her egg on a spoon, and she tripped over her shoelaces. She fell face-first right onto her egg. She literally had egg all over her face. It was supermessy and supergross," Alexis finished.

Emma shuddered. "It was so sticky and disgusting! And everyone was laughing at me. It was awful."

"But you were just an uncoordinated third grader back then," I said. "I bet you'd do just fine if you did it today."

"Can I switch with Emma? I'd rather do the egg race than wear a sweatshirt," Mia said.

I shook my head. I was enjoying this. "No way. It has to be something that counts. Only then will you know how I truly feel inside about this cupcake issue."

Mia turned to Alexis. "What about you?"

"I still can't think of anything," Alexis replied.

"I know!" I cried out. "Alexis, you hate spicy food, right? So you have to eat something spicy."

Alexis made a face. "Seriously? You want me to risk a painful mouth burn for you?"

"You cannot burn your mouth eating spicy food," I said.

"Oh yes, you can," Alexis insisted. "The oils in those spicy peppers can really mess you up."

"How about medium spicy, then?" Mia suggested. "One step above mild."

Alexis looked like she was going to protest, but Emma nudged her.

"All right," Alexis said with a sigh. "I'll do it. This means we can do the peanut-butter-and-guava-jelly cupcakes, right?"

"Right," I said, and suddenly the idea didn't seem too scary anymore. I guess change isn't so bad as long as your friends have to change along with you.

CHAPTER 8

Mia's Fashion Splash

The next morning Mia went to stay with her dad in Manhattan, but I made sure she didn't forget her end of our deal.

Don't forget 2 wear ur sweatshirt 2morrow, I texted her on Sunday.

Nooooooooooo! Mia replied. But I knew she would do it. Mia is the kind of friend who keeps her promises.

So when I got on the bus to school on Monday morning, I wasn't disappointed. Mia was sitting in her usual seat in the sixth row, wearing a blue "I ♥ NY" sweatshirt. She looked miserable.

"Mia, you did it!" I said happily, sliding into the seat next to her.

Mia looked down at herself, sighing. "I don't even own a sweatshirt, so my dad bought this for me at the train station before I came home. I hope you don't mind, but it looked so awful that I had to change it a little bit."

"Really? I didn't even notice," I said.

"Well, the long sleeves were really too hot for spring, so I cut them off and then made pockets out of them. I also fixed the neckline a little bit," she explained.

Then I saw what she had done. The short sleeves were pushed up and attached with silver buttons. The neckline was more of a V shape, and the pockets in front looked kind of cute. Mia had layered the shirt over a thin white one with long sleeves. She had rolled the bottom of her jeans above her white sneakers, and she had pulled her hair back into a sporty ponytail.

"It looks really nice," I said. "You could make anything look good, Mia."

Mia smiled a little. "Thanks. But I still cannot believe that I am going to school in a *sweatshirt*!"

Poor Mia. I knew this was hard for her. That just goes to show you what an awesome friend she is!

Alexis and Emma were waiting for us on the front steps when the bus pulled up.

"Wow, Mia, you did it!" Emma said. "I think you look great."

Mia looked around. "Everyone is staring at me; I know it!"

"If they are, it's just because you look good," I said.

Alexis rolled her eyes. "Mia, you have it so easy! At least you don't have to risk injuring yourself."

"By eating delicious food? You don't know how lucky you are," Mia shot back. "At least you don't have to do your new thing in front of the whole school!"

We went inside, and Emma and I went to our homeroom. I saw Mia again after that, during math class with Mr. Kazinski, and she seemed a little better. She was even happier during third-period gym class.

"Finally, I'm out of that sweatshirt!" she said, looking down at her T-shirt and shorts. "I'm free!"

Ms. Chen, our gym teacher, blew her whistle. "Line up, everybody! Let's get moving!"

I once got the nerve to ask Ms. Chen if she had ever been in the military, because she runs the class like an army commander. (I left that second part out.) She claimed she hadn't, so I guess she was just born that way. Sometimes it can make gym class very stressful, depending on what we're doing.

After we did some jumping jacks and squat thrusts. Ms. Chen made us count off ("One! Two! One! Two!") and divide into two teams. I like it when she does that, because then nobody has to get picked last (usually, it's me).

Ms. Chen set up some orange cones. "We're going to do relay races today. I want each team to line up behind a cone."

I was kind of relieved to hear that we were doing relay races. I stink at a lot of sports, but I'm a pretty good runner. I had been a number two, so I lined up with my other teammates. I'm lucky that all my good friends are in my gym class, so I'm usually never alone on a team. This time, I was on a team with Alexis and George.

Everybody raced to line up behind the cone, and I ended up last. I started to panic a little. In a relay race, winning or losing often depends on the very last runner.

"Hey!" I called to George, who was in the middle of the line. "Shouldn't somebody else be last?"

George smiled at me. "Don't worry, Katie. You can do it!"

I anxiously looked over at the other line and

was surprised to see Callie in last place. She and I used to be best friends since we were babies. But now she's head of the BFC, and we don't talk much anymore. Callie plays sports, so she's pretty fast. I started to get nervous all over again.

"Ready, set, go!" Ms. Chen yelled.

The first runner from each team took off across the gym, circled the cone at the far end, and then ran back, tagging the next runner. Things were moving pretty quickly, and I knew my turn was coming up soon.

The teams were pretty much even. George ran and then stopped by me on his way to the back of the line.

"Just stay focused," he advised. "Don't look at the other person running."

I nodded. "Okay, coach."

Then it was Alexis's turn, and my heart was pounding. She rounded the cone and then came back and tagged me just as Maggie, another member of the BFC, tagged Callie.

Don't look at her, I reminded myself, and I took off as fast as I could. I stayed focused, and I could feel my legs moving faster and faster. *All that running I've been doing with Mom is paying off,* I thought, *because I'm a better runner than I was last year.*

I ran back to the cone and slapped the hand of the first person on line. Suddenly, my team started cheering.

It was like I was in a daze or something. I looked at the other team and saw Callie slap her teammate's hand just seconds after I had finished.

"We won! We won!" Alexis cried, hugging me.

I couldn't believe it! I'm not using to winning at stuff, especially in gym. George came up and high-fived me.

"I told you you'd be great!" he said. "I hope you're on my team on Spirit Day!"

I know I blushed a little, and Alexis nudged me.

"He soooo likes you," she whispered. Alexis might be the most serious of all my friends, but she's also the most boy-crazy, too.

"I don't care if he does or not," I said. "I'm just glad he's my friend." Which was kind of a lie. Inside, it feels kind of good to think that a boy likes me, especially a nice one like George. But I'm not good at talking about it, not even with Mia or Alexis.

After gym we have lunch, which is okay except sometimes it's gross to eat when you're hot and sweaty. But all that running had made me hungry, and I was happy to eat the P-B-and-J sandwich and carrot sticks that Mom had packed for me.

Mia was next to me, eating some yogurt, when she suddenly put down her spoon.

"Oh no," she said. "The BFC is talking about me!"

We all looked over at the BFC's table. The members of the Best Friends Club are Callie, Maggie, Bella, and Olivia, the new girl who I told you about who made friends with Mia. They kept looking over at our table and then looking at one another and whispering.

"Maybe they are, but you never cared about that before," I said.

"Well, I never wore a *sweatshirt* before," Mia said. "They're probably talking about what a dork I look like."

Alexis scowled. "Let them come over here and say something to your face."

"Honestly, I think you look nice," Emma said. "Kind of sporty chic, like the way we dressed for my brothers' party."

"Yeah, the one where Olivia ended up covered in cupcakes," I said, and we laughed, remembering. Even Mia was smiling.

"Yeah, I guess that *is* a little more embarrassing than wearing a sweatshirt," Mia admitted. "But I'll still be glad when this day is over."

By the end of the day, Mia didn't even mention the sweatshirt anymore, so I guess she made peace with the whole thing. She didn't say a word about it on the bus. When I got home, I did my homework until Mom came back from work.

"Did you have a good day today, Katie?" she asked me.

"Yeah," I replied. "My team in gym won the relay race, and I was the last runner, so that was pretty cool."

"Wow, that's great!" Mom said. She reached into the refrigerator and took out a package of ground beef. "I'm going to make some meat loaf for dinner, okay?"

Mom's meat loaf is okay, but it's not my favorite. "Couldn't we make tacos instead?" I asked.

Mom frowned. "We could, but I don't have any taco shells in the cupboard, and I think we're out of lettuce, too."

"Pretty please?" I asked in my sweetest voice. (Yes, I was still taking advantage of Mom's good mood. But wouldn't you if tacos were at stake?)

"Okay," Mom said with a smile. She grabbed her car keys from the counter. "Back in a flash!"

I started to feel a little guilty as she left, so I made up for it by emptying the dishwasher and setting the table without being asked. I'm not all bad! After dinner Mom and I went for a run together, and there was no sign of the guy in the blue sweatsuit. I was starting to hope that maybe the whole thing was over. But then again, she was still wearing lip gloss, so I wasn't sure.

The next morning Mia was in a much better mood when I got on the bus. She had gotten pretty dolled up in a dress with a pink and purple flower pattern, and a black belt around her waist. She had her hair down, and long, dangly silver earrings in her ears.

"Wow, you look nice," I said.

"I wanted to burn the sweatshirt the minute I got home from school yesterday, but Eddie said we have to wait until we set up the fire pit this summer," Mia said. "I am so happy to be back to normal."

After we got off the bus, we were heading to the front steps to meet up with Alexis and Emma when I noticed the BFC walking down the street together. I couldn't believe my eyes.

I poked Mia. "You'd better look at this."

Mia turned and her eyes got wide. Every member of the BFC was wearing a sweatshirt and jeans, just like Mia had the day before! They had changed their sweatshirts too, cutting off the sleeves and adding the pockets and stuff. They all had their hair pulled back into ponytails.

"You know what?" Mia said. "They actually look pretty cute."

"We tried to tell you," I said.

The BFC walked by us. Callie looked in our direction and nodded.

"Hi, Katie. Hi, Mia."

"Hi, Callie," I said. "Like your outfit."

Callie smiled, and the girls kept moving. I turned to Mia, shaking my head and laughing.

"I guess you *are* a real trendsetter," I told her.

Mia smiled. "Hmm. Maybe I won't burn that sweatshirt after all. It's an original design!"

CHAPTER 9

Things Suddenly Get Weird

We got together at my house after school on Wednesday for a special Cupcake Club meeting. Mom was in her home office, doing some stuff on her computer, and the Cupcake Club was in the kitchen, working on a display idea for the PTA dinner.

Mia had out her sketchbook. "Okay, so maybe we should first figure out how to decorate the cupcakes. The icing is pale brown, which is not exactly exciting."

"Well, we're doing a twist on classic pairs. Maybe we could do two hands shaking or something?" I suggested.

Mia frowned. "Hands are hard to do, especially if we're cutting them out of fondant." Fondant is a sort of dough you make out of sugar, and you can use it to make decorations for your cupcakes and cakes. We use it sometimes, but it's not my favorite way to decorate our cupcakes. Mia and Emma are the best at working with it.

"We could write 'PTA' on them, or 'PSMS' for 'Park Street Middle School,'" Alexis said.

Mia started sketching. "Not bad. But not supercreative, either."

Emma spoke up. "I like it when the decorations are done with food in a pretty way, you know? Like an edible flower."

Mia nodded. "That could be nice."

"Ooh, I know!" I said. "We could pick something that goes with the peanut butter and guava flavors. Like maybe some candied ginger."

"Isn't that spicy?" Alexis asked worriedly.

"A little, but when it's candied, it's mostly sweet," I said. I took out my phone and then started to look for a picture to show everyone. "See? It's pretty, like a little jewel or something."

Everyone gathered around my phone. "That's really nice," Mia said. "Understated, but classy."

Alexis nodded. "I could see that appealing to the PTA parents. And it's unusual."

"I'll pick some up the next time I go back to

that gourmet shop in town," Emma volunteered. "It's fun in there."

"Can I go with you?" I asked. "I haven't been yet."

"Sure," Emma replied.

Just then I heard a ping on my phone. It was an e-mail. I don't get a lot of those; mostly texts from my friends. Sometimes Grandma Carole sends me photos by e-mail, so I opened up the e-mail screen.

"It's from someone named Marc Donald," I said, reading the name in my in-box. "But I don't know any Marc Donald."

"Ooh! Maybe it's from a secret admirer," Alexis teased.

I blushed. "I don't have one. It's probably just spam."

"Or maybe it's George Martinez, using a fake name," Emma said.

"Well, it's definitely from a boy," Mia chimed in. "Open it!"

I was curious, and moved to push the button to read new messages.

"No, wait, don't!" Alexis cried out. "Remember all that stuff we learned about online safety? Your mom will kill you. Besides, it's not George, see? The whole address is marcdonald@thebrowns.com."

"The Browns?" Mia asked. "That's your last

name. Maybe it's a cousin or something."

I thought about it, but I don't have any cousins or uncles named Marc. "I don't think so," I said, shaking my head.

"Maybe it's someone who did one of those family tree things online, and they tracked you down!" Emma said excitedly.

"One way to found out," I said. "MOM!"

Mom came into the kitchen, frowning. "We do not yell in this house, Katie. This is not a football stadium."

"Sorry," I said. "It's just, I got an e-mail from a boy I don't know, and I didn't want to open it."

Mom smiled. "Well, that was smart. Now I know I can trust you with your e-mail." She raised her eyebrows. "So, a boy, huh?"

I handed her my phone, and her smile immediately faded. She turned pale. "Oh," she said. "Maybe we can open this later, Katie."

"Why later?" I asked, more curious than ever. "Is it a long-lost relative or something?"

"Sort of," Mom answered. "Let's read it later."

"Come on, please!" I begged. The suspense was too much. "I really want to know."

Mom nervously looked around the room. "Why don't you come into my office?"

I shot a questioning look at my friends, but followed Mom out of the kitchen. I was starting to feel a little nervous. What was the big deal about the e-mail?

As soon as we got into her office, I asked, "Mom, do you know who Marc Donald is?"

Mom took a deep breath. "Katie, Marc Donald is your dad."

I was shocked. That didn't make sense at all. "But Dad's name is Donald, and the e-mail was from *Marc* Donald."

"His full name is Marc Donald Brown. He's always gone by Donald, though," Mom replied. She and I stared at each other for a little bit. Obviously, the situation was weird for both of us.

"So, what does he want?" I finally asked.

"I'm not sure," Mom confessed. "Why don't you have fun with your friends? I'll read the e-mail, and we'll talk about it after they leave, okay?"

This was the first time in weeks I'd seen Mom looking unhappy. I realized I wasn't so curious to find out what was in the e-mail anymore. I didn't feel excited—just weird.

I went back into the kitchen, and my friends pounced on me.

"Who was it? A boy?" Mia asked.

"No," I said, and then I just blurted it out. "It's my dad."

Everyone got really quiet. I barely ever talk about my dad. Mia knows more than Emma and Alexis do, and even she doesn't know that much.

"When was the last time you saw him?" Alexis asked.

"My mom says I was about two," I explained. "He left, and he moved across the country and then started this whole other family. He used to send me a Christmas card every year, but I stopped getting them recently."

Emma's eyes got wide. "Do you mean you have brothers and sisters who you've never met?" She looked really upset, and I could tell she was thinking about her own brothers.

Mia put her hand on my shoulder. "I'm sorry, Katie. This must be hard."

"It's more . . . strange," I said. "I mean, he's never been a part of my life, so what does he want now? I'm kind of curious."

"Do you remember anything about him?" Alexis asked.

I shook my head. "Not really. I can't even picture him in my head, and Mom only has one photo of him holding me when I was a baby."

"Well, it's a good sign he's reaching out, right?" Emma reasoned. "Maybe he wants to come see you."

I tried to imagine seeing my dad, in person, but I just couldn't picture it. What would I even say to him?

"I wonder what he's like," I mused, changing the subject. "I mean, I know he went to dental school with Mom, but I think she told me he's not a dentist anymore."

"Maybe he's got a cool job, like a musician or something," Mia suggested.

"Or a movie producer," Alexis added.

"Maybe," I said quietly.

All I knew was that I was feeling pretty confused about everything.

CHAPTER 10

"Your Dad, Marc Donald Brown"

$\mathcal{I}$t didn't take us long to finish up our plan for the PTA display. When my friends left, I found Mom in her bedroom, reading a book.

"Mom, I think I want to read that e-mail now," I said.

Mom nodded, but she didn't look happy. "Okay. Let's read it together."

For a second I almost argued with her. It was *my* e-mail, wasn't it? Why did she have to be so protective? But I was really eager to see the e-mail, so I didn't make a big deal out of it.

I looked over Mom's shoulder as she opened the e-mail on my phone, and I read the message silently to myself. My heart started to beat really fast, though I wasn't exactly sure why.

Dear Katie,

I know it's been a very long time since I've seen you, but I think of you often. I live nearby with my wife and our three children, and I'd like very much to come take you to lunch or for ice cream, so we can get to know each other a little more. Here is my e-mail address, my home address, and my phone number.

Love,

Your dad, Marc Donald Brown

"Your dad, Marc Donald Brown." For some reason, that line stuck with me. I mean, I know that Marc Donald Brown is my father. But a dad is more than a father, right? Like Callie's dad, who used to play Monopoly with us for hours; or Alexis's dad, who drives us places; or even Mia's stepdad, who cooks for us and makes jokes. How could Marc Donald Brown say he's my dad?

Unless maybe he wants to be my dad now, I thought, and I could feel a tiny spark of hope shimmer inside me. I think a part of me had been wishing for that my whole life.

"You okay, Katie?" Mom asked softly. She chewed her lip, like she does when she's upset.

"I want to e-mail him back, Mom," I said.

Mom looked surprised. "You do?"

I nodded.

Mom looked thoughtful. "Look, Katie, I don't want to see you get hurt. Please let me call him first and talk about what his intentions are with you. He left us a very long time ago, and this is the first time he's reached out like this. I guess I don't trust him. I need to find out what's going on or what has changed to make him do this."

That sounded fair. But one thing was still bugging me.

"Mom, he says he lives nearby—look at his address. It's one town over! I thought you said he moved to Washington."

"He did, at first," Mom said. "But then he moved back here with his family a few years ago. I didn't tell you because . . . Well, I'm not sure why, honestly. I kept worrying that would we run in to him somewhere, but we never did."

It took a minute for this all to sink in. I couldn't be mad with Mom for not telling me. Even if I knew, what would I have done? Knocked on his front door and said, "Hello, I'm your long-lost daughter, Katie?"

"What about those kids he has?" I asked. "Are they boys or girls? Do you know how old they are?"

Mom shook her head. "I'm not sure. We've never talked about that stuff."

I thought about it a little longer.

"So those kids are my half siblings?" I asked.

"Yes, they are," Mom replied.

I was almost more curious about the kids than I was about my dad. I've always liked being an only child, but sometimes I think it would be nice to have a sister. (Just one, because as you know, when I'm around lots of kids, I sometimes freak out.) But Dad had three children, he'd written. Were they boys? Then I'd have three brothers, just like Emma. If they were girls, I'd have more sisters than any of my friends. And would they look like me? *Probably not,* I thought, *because I look a lot like my mom.*

"Katie, you look tired," Mom said. "Why don't you take a shower and then get ready for bed?"

"Okay, Mom," I replied. I did what she said, but as soon as I was done, I closed the door to my bedroom and called Mia, even though it was late.

"Can you talk?" I asked in a loud whisper.

"Sure," Mia said. "Are you okay?"

"I guess," I said. "I mean, this whole thing with my dad is weird. He says he wants to see me. But Mom won't let me e-mail him back until she talks to him. I still don't know anything about him."

"Did you google him?" Mia asked.

I slapped my hand to my forehead. Why hadn't I thought of that?

"Let me do it now," I murmured.

I used my laptop, so I could google and talk to Mia at the same time. I typed in "Marc Donald Brown" and then "Stonebrook," the name of the town he lives in.

"Oh my gosh," I hissed. "Mia, he owns a restaurant in Stonebrook called Chez Donald."

"No way!" Mia said. "My mom and Eddie go there sometimes. I bet they've seen him, and they didn't even know he was your dad! How weird is that?"

"Superextra weird," I said. "I still can't believe he's so close."

"Well, the restaurant part makes sense," Mia says. "I mean, you love to cook."

That part didn't hit me until Mia said it. "Well, Mom likes to cook too. So I must get it from both of them."

"You know," Mia said, "we could go to the restaurant, and, like, check him out."

"I don't know," I replied. Even though Mom was being overprotective, I kind of didn't mind.

Things were changing pretty fast. One minute, no dad; the next minute, a dad and three half siblings. Getting used to guava jelly was one thing, but I wasn't sure about this whole dad thing.

CHAPTER II

Emma and the Egg

"Welcome to Spirit Day, everyone!"

Principal LaCosta stood on the bleachers on the school field, talking through a megaphone. It was Friday morning, and Spirit Day had finally arrived. All the kids in my grade were milling about on the field, standing with our homerooms and waiting to find out our team assignments.

Since Emma is in my homeroom, she and I were standing together. She was nervously looking over at the pile of game equipment on the grass just in front of the bleachers.

"I definitely see a bucket of eggs," she said with a grimace. "Rats! I was hoping I could get away with doing something else."

"You're going to be fine," I assured her. "You've

got way more balance than you did in third grade."

"Maybe," Emma said. "But anything could happen. Anything!"

"The worst thing that could happen is that you'll get egg on you," I said. "And if you do, so what?"

Emma sighed. "I guess."

We were interrupted by Mr. Kazinski, our homeroom teacher.

"All right! When I call your name, please come up and take the stick that I give you. Then find people with the same color stick, and that's your team."

We all eagerly lined up. Emma was in front of me, and she got a light blue stick.

"Fingers crossed," she said to me.

But the stick I got was dark pink—I guess you would call it fuchsia. Emma frowned. "Too bad. I hope we get to be on teams with nice people."

"Me too," I said. "I guess we'd better find them."

We walked around, waving our sticks, when we saw Alexis holding a green one. She made a big sad face and pointed to it. Then we heard Mia call out, "Katie! Emma! Alexis! Did anyone get purple?"

I turned and saw her running toward us. "No! I'm fuchsia!"

"Is that what this color is?" George Martinez walked up from behind me, carrying a fuchsia stick. "I just thought it was pink. Anyway, looks like we're on the same team."

"Yeah," I said, smiling. From the corner of my eyes, I saw Mia smirk at me.

"Let's go find everyone else," George said, and I waved to my friends as we took off.

It didn't take long to find our other team members. There were ten people on a team, and I sort of knew most everyone. I knew George the best, and then there was my friend Sophie, who's really cool. And then there's Chau, who's in my English class. I don't know him very well, but whenever we have to write poems, his are always the funniest and the most well written.

George was counting us. "Eight . . . nine . . . Hey, we're one short!"

"Maybe somebody got fuchsia mixed up with purple," Sophie said. "They're kind of close in color."

I started to look around to spot the other fuchsia stick when I heard a whiny voice behind me.

"This is, like, the lamest thing ever. Do we really have to do this?"

I'd know that voice anywhere. It was Olivia. I

noticed she was wearing skinny jeans, a lacy white top, and sandals with a wedge heel—not exactly the best thing to wear on Spirit Day.

George got right to the point. "Hey, Number Ten! What are you wearing those shoes for? Didn't anyone tell you to wear sneakers?"

Olivia dramatically rolled her eyes. "Like I care. In my old town we stopped doing this kind of thing in elementary school. You guys can do the races or whatever. I'll cheer or something."

George shrugged. "Whatever." Then he raised his voice. "All right, Team Fuchsia! Let's get it together!"

George is the kind of kid who's almost always captain when he's on a team. But he's not bossy or anything, and when I'm on a team with him, I end up having fun. I had a feeling this was going to be good, even with Olivia complaining the whole time.

The first thing we had to do wasn't a race or anything. First, all the teams had to come up with a team name and make a banner.

"George already said we were Team Fuchsia," Sophia pointed out.

"We can't do the color as our name," chirped up a kid named John. "That would be boring."

"How about Team Kung-Fu? That still has 'fu' in it," George suggested.

"Team Kung-Fu Weasels!" Chau said, and just about everyone laughed (everyone but Olivia, who still looked miserable).

"Kung-Fu Weasel Warriors!" I added, and everyone liked it.

"Katie, that is awesome!" George crowed. "So who knows how to draw a weasel?"

Sophie raised her hand. "I think I can. It's like a ferret, right?"

We all shrugged. Nobody knew for sure, but that sounded close enough.

"Just make it fuchsia," said Tina, this girl from my science class.

So we all gathered around the big paper banner and art supplies we'd been given and made the banner. I can do pretty cool bubble letters, so I did the team name, and then the other kids colored them in. Sophie's weasel came out awesome, and even Olivia got into it, drawing little fuchsia hearts everywhere.

"Love it!" I praised when we were done.

"Let's hang it up," George said.

We took the banner to the fence and then hung it up with string. All the banners looked pretty cool all together. Mia's purple team had called themselves the Raging Cannonballs, and there was a great drawing of a cannon on their banner that I'm sure Mia had made. Alexis and the green team were Team Slytherin, and Emma and the light blue team were the Kangaroo Commandos. They were all great names, but I liked Kung-Fu Weasel Warriors the best.

Ms. Chen blew a whistle. "Teams! Line up for the over-and-under relay!"

In case you've never played it, the over-and-under relay is when the first person in line gives the ball to the second person by passing it to him or her from between their own legs, and then the second person has to pass it by reaching over their own head, and then the third person has to pass it under, and so on. But when we lined up and Ms. Chen passed out the balls, we saw there was a twist: The balls were water balloons!

I was between Sophie and Olivia in the middle of the line.

"Be careful passing it to me, Silly Arms," Olivia said to me, using a nickname I'd got in gym class. "I don't want to get this shirt wet. It's new!"

I was in a good mood, so Olivia's name-calling didn't even bother me. I wiggled my eyebrows at her. "Anything can happen on Spirit Day, Olivia. But I'll do my best."

The whistle blew, and then everyone started yelling as the race began. Soon I saw Sophie reaching between her legs to pass the balloon to me, and I bent down to scoop it up. Then I reached over my head and all the way back.

"All yours, Olivia!" I called.

Olivia grabbed it from me, and I turned around to see the rest of the race. Our team was doing pretty well. At the end of the line, Chau handed the balloon over his head to George, and we heard a whistle blow.

"Kung-Fu Weasel Warriors are first!" Ms. Chen cried.

We all started cheering, and George held up the balloon like he was going to throw it. We shrieked and laughed, and George threw the balloon right into our midst. Nobody got soaked, but the cool splash of water felt good. I looked over at Olivia, and she was smiling and laughing and not freaking out at all.

We played a bunch more games. There was this one where you see which member of your team can throw a rubber chicken the farthest; another one where you see who can twirl a hula-hoop the longest; and there was a three-legged race I did with Sophie, and we came in second place, which was pretty cool. Then it was time for the egg race.

"Okay, we need four volunteers from each team," Ms. Chen announced, and I looked over at the light blue team. True to her word, Emma raised her hand. I raised my hand for my team, and I saw Mia and Alexis raise theirs too. We weren't going to let Emma do this alone.

Amazingly, it worked out so that me, Emma, Alexis, and Mia were all last for our teams. The race started, and George went first, and then Tina, and then Chau. Chau walked the course, and when he handed me the spoon with the egg on it, he said, "That was egg-cellent!"

I started to carefully walk toward the cone down the field, balancing my egg. So far, a few teams had lost their eggs, but all the Cupcake Club members were still in the race. I looked over at Emma, and she was going superslow, and she was a little bit sweaty. But she was doing it!

"You can do it, Emma!" I cheered as I passed her.

Then we rounded the cones. Alexis was moving more quickly than any of us. She got back to her team first and won the race for Team Slytherin. Mia got back to her team just a step or two before I did. Then we all turned to watch Emma.

Her cheeks were bright red, because now everyone in our grade was looking at her. Her hand started to shake a little bit, and for a minute I got worried. But she didn't take her eyes off the egg for one second. Slowly and carefully, she made it across the finish line.

"Team Kangaroo Commandos brings it home for fourth place!" Ms. Chen announced.

Mia, Alexis, and I ran over to Emma then and started screaming and hugging her. As I went in to squeeze her, I realized she was still holding the egg in her spoon. In slow motion, I watched as the egg dropped from the spoon and hit the grass. . . .

And then sat there. Confused, I bent down to touch it. It was hard-boiled!

I picked it up and showed it to Emma. "Looks like you didn't have anything to worry about," I said, and then Emma started cracking up.

"No way!" she said. "Why didn't they do that in elementary school? I feel so silly. But I'm glad that's over with!"

We went back to our teams and played a few more games. In the end, Team Slytherin had the most points, but nobody really cared who won or lost. We were all really having fun.

At the end of the games, they brought out boxes of pizza, and everyone sat on the bleachers, chowing down. Mia, Alexis, and Emma came to sit with me, and Sophie's best friend, Lucy, came to sit with her. Callie, Maggie, and Bella from the BFC wandered over to sit by Olivia. Ken sat with George and Chau, and then Eddie went over to talk to Maggie. Everybody was chattering and laughing.

"Hey, we should go to the park after this," George said.

I knew we were going to be dismissed from school right after the pizza, but I figured I'd just get on the bus and then go home, like always. I sometimes go to my friends' houses after school, but I've never done the hanging out thing.

I looked at Mia questioningly.

"We should do it," she said.

I took out my phone. "I should text my mom."

Going to go to park after school with some friends. K?

Who? Mom texted back. (I told you she was overprotective, remember?)

Mia, Alexis, Emma, and a bunch of other kids.

K. Be home by 5, Mom texted back.

And so that's how I found myself hanging at the park with my three best friends, the BFC, Sophie and Lucy, and a bunch of boys. We went on the swing sets and walked around, and then we all sat in the grass around the pond, talking and stuff.

This was definitely a new thing—guava-jelly new, even. Boys and girls together, like it was no big deal. Old friends and new friends and best friends and sometimes friends. Definitely different, but it felt really good.

And then I got to thinking that maybe whoever organized Spirit Day knew what they were doing after all.

And then I thought of Mom and her secret boyfriend, and my father and his strange e-mail.

Maybe sometimes, change is good, I thought, *but not all the time!*

CHAPTER 12

A Big Decision

That night Mom ordered Chinese food for us. I like to use chopsticks when I eat Chinese food, because it's more fun. I'm still not great at using them yet, so I ordered tofu and broccoli. (I could pick up the big chunks more easily.)

"Katie, we should make cupcakes tonight," Mom suggested.

"Are you sure you don't want to go running all by yourself?" I asked, and inside I cringed as soon as the words came out. I know it was kind of mean of me to ask her that way, but I swear sometimes words just come out of me and I can't stop them.

But Mom didn't look upset or anything. "I'd rather stay here with you—unless you're tired of making cupcakes?"

"Now *that* is a ridiculous question," I said with a grin.

"So what kind should we make?" Mom asked.

I thought for a minute. "How about peanut butter and jelly?"

"Aren't you doing that with the Cupcake Club?"

"I mean, peanut butter and *grape* jelly," I said. "You know, the original recipe. Just like the ones you always make me for the first day of school or when I have a big test or something."

Mom smiled. "Let's do it."

Soon, we were in the kitchen, and Mom let me blast the radio loud. Before we knew it, we were baking and talking, and I ended up telling her all about Spirit Day and the park and stuff. After a few hours we were sitting at the kitchen table, biting into the finished cupcakes, which were still slightly warm. The peanut-butter icing was smooth and creamy, and the grape jelly inside was an awesome burst of grapeness.

"I forgot how good these are," Mom remarked. "I guess they are like good, old, comfort cupcakes."

"They're the best," I agreed.

Mom put down her cupcake and then gave me one of those supersweet mom looks. "I love you, Peanut Butter," she said.

I laughed. "I love you too, Jelly."

I guess I should explain. When I was in nursery school, I told my teacher my mom and I were like peanut butter and jelly, because we went everywhere together. I guess that shows you how close my mom and I have always been.

"The PTA is going to love these," Mom raved.

"Oh, I thought you knew," I said. "We're not doing grape jelly. We're doing guava jelly with some candied ginger on top for decoration."

"That actually sounds very good," Mom said.

I sighed. "I was totally against the guava. I got mad at everybody for wanting to change it. So do you know what they did? They each agreed to try something new, just for me. That's why Emma did the egg race today. And Mia even wore a sweatshirt to school!"

Mom laughed. "Oh my gosh, she did? She must really love you."

"And Alexis is going to eat spicy food," I told her. I giggled. "I can't wait to see that."

"Well, it's good to try new things," Mom said. "Even classic recipes have to be tweaked once in a while. The jelly might be different, but it's still a P-B-and-J cupcake."

"I guess you're right," I admitted. We quietly ate

our cupcakes for the next few minutes, licking the icing. (We even eat cupcakes the same way.)

Mom broke the silence. "I spoke to your father," she said, and I got a little chill. Half of me had been dying for the past few days, wondering if Mom had talked to him, and the other half had been hoping the whole thing had been forgotten.

"What did he say?" I asked casually.

"Well, he wants to get to know you," Mom started. "I asked him what sparked the e-mail, but he didn't really say. And I let him know that I would have appreciated it if he had contacted me first. I still have some concerns, but I'd like to know how you feel. Would you like to see him, Katie?"

Suddenly, everything was totally real, and I started to feel panicked. What if we met and I didn't like him? Or he didn't like me? Or his kids didn't like me? This decision was way bigger than guava jelly.

"I'm not sure," I replied honestly.

"That's okay," Mom said, putting her arm around me. "There's no rush—as far as I'm concerned, anyway. You take your time, Katie. When you make up your mind, let me know. Do you have any questions or concerns that you want to talk about?"

I did, but everything was all jumbled up in my

brain, so I just shook my head. Mom gave me a little hug.

Then I thought of a question I *did* want to ask—about Mom's secret boyfriend. But I didn't want to ruin the moment. Things felt really good—just me and Mom eating cupcakes. So what if it wasn't new and exciting? It's exactly where I wanted to be.

CHAPTER 13

Alexis Heats Up

Dinner 2-nite at my house, Mia texted me the next morning. Alexis is going to do the spicy thing.

Cool! Let me ask Mom, I replied.

She was in another humming/lip gloss mood that morning, so of course she said yes. In fact, she got on the phone and came back and said, "I talked to Mia's mom. She said you can stay until ten. I'll pick you up then."

"Let me guess," I said. "You're going out to dinner with some friends, right?"

Mom looked at me funny. "Just one friend, actually." And then she quickly left the room.

I was glad Mia invited me over, because between my father and my mother, I was feeling pretty confused. Watching Alexis try to eat spicy food would definitely take my mind off things.

When I got to Mia's, a delicious smell was wafting throughout the house. Alexis was already there with Mia.

"Where's Emma?" I asked. Since Emma and Alexis live close to each other, they usually arrive everywhere at the same time.

"She had to take Jake to a T-ball game," Alexis explained. "She'll be here soon."

I nodded toward the kitchen. "That smells sooo good. What's on the menu?"

Mia made a face. "I'm not sure. Eddie's been in there for hours."

"Let's find out," I said.

"Let's not," Alexis said worriedly. "I'd rather not know."

I grabbed her arm. "Come on, just looking won't hurt."

But when we got to the kitchen, Eddie shooed us away. "Out! Out! I am creating a masterpiece here. I need complete concentration."

We left the kitchen, giggling.

"He's taking this pretty seriously," I noted.

"I hope not *too* seriously," Alexis muttered. She looked miserable.

Then the doorbell rang.

"That must be Emma," Mia guessed. But when she opened the door, we saw it wasn't just Emma— her brother Matt was with her.

"He insisted on coming along," Emma said, rolling her eyes. "I hope you don't mind."

Behind her, Matt shrugged off the insult. "I love spicy food and Dad hates it, so we never have it at our house," he said. "Plus, I want to see if Alexis will really go through with it."

"No problem. Let me ask Eddie if you can stay," Mia said. She raised her voice. "Eddie! Is it okay if Matt eats with us?"

"Of course!" Eddie yelled back. "The more the merrier!"

"I'm going to go through with it!" Alexis mumbled huffily, but she still looked nervous, although slightly less miserable. She's always had kind of a crush on Matt, who's one year older than us. I think he must like Alexis too—at least a little bit. He agreed to be her partner in the pep-rally parade. He's got blond hair and blue eyes, just like Emma, and he's really cute. But Emma thinks he's totally annoying.

"So, you really like spicy food?" Alexis asked.

Matt nodded. "It's awesome! I once ate Indian

food, and my head was sweating so much, I couldn't believe it. Totally gross, but the food was worth it."

Alexis was really getting fidgety. "You don't think Eddie is making head-sweating food, do you?"

"I don't know," Mia replied. "But he did bring back a big bag of peppers from the grocery store."

Mia's stepbrother, Dan, came down the stairs. "Yo," he said, nodding toward Matt. Dan and Emma's oldest brother, Sam, know each other, and sometimes they all get together to play basketball. Then Dan nodded toward Mia. "Dinner ready yet?"

"I'm not sure," Mia answered.

Then Mia's mom came into the living room, wearing a bright red dress. "Eddie says it's time for the spicy feast to begin, everybody," she announced. She smiled at Matt. "I've set an extra place for you."

"Awesome. Thanks." Matt was happy. "My mouth is watering."

"Wow, Mrs. Valdes," I said. "That's a really red dress! I mean, it's nice, but it's *really* red."

Mia's mom smiled. "A spicy meal calls for a spicy dress. Come on, let's go to the dining room."

Mia's mom and stepdad had decorated the dining room with a bright red tablecloth, red napkins, and red glasses to go with their usual set of white dinner plates. We took our seats, and I noticed Alexis slid into the one next to Matt.

Eddie came into the dining room, carrying a steaming platter of food in each hand.

"Fried plantains," he said, placing down the first platter. And then, "Yellow rice."

"These aren't spicy," Mia remarked.

"Spicy, coming right up!" Eddie said. He disappeared into the kitchen and then returned with a large silver platter filled with golden pieces of chicken, covered in a green sauce.

"Spicy marinated chicken with green chile sauce," Eddie announced proudly.

Matt inhaled the scent. "Oh man, that smells good."

"Pass me your plates," Mrs. Valdes instructed, standing up. "The platters are kind of heavy."

Soon we each had a plate full of chicken, sauce, rice, and plantains. My stomach was growling.

We began to eat. I have to admit that I was a tiny bit hesitant about eating the spicy chicken. I mean, I like spicy, but this looked *really* spicy. So I ate some plantains first, to warm up. They're kind of like big bananas that aren't as sweet, and they're crispy and creamy when they're fried. Then I took a tiny bite of the chicken and sauce. It was delicious—but definitely hot! I quickly ate a forkful of rice to counteract the heat.

Unfortunately, Alexis saw my expression. "Oh my gosh, Katie, look at your face!" she said, pointing. "I love you, but I don't think I can do this. Maybe I can do another challenge."

"Come on, Alexis," Matt coaxed her. "You can do it. It's not so bad, I swear." He touched her hand for a split second, and Alexis blushed.

Alexis sighed and then picked up her fork. I knew she wouldn't back down in front of Matt.

"Okay," she relented. She carefully cut a little square of chicken about the size of a quarter, and dipped a tiny corner of it in the sauce. Then she slowly, slowly, brought the fork to her mouth.

Every eye in the room was on Alexis, and nobody said a word as she put the chicken into her mouth. She chewed, she swallowed, and then—

"Aaaauuuuggghh!" she shrieked. She quickly grabbed a glass of water and then gulped it down.

"Don't do that!" Eddie warned. "The water will just spread the oil of the chilies around in your mouth. It'll make it worse."

Alexis grimaced. "I just figured that out."

Eddie jumped up and then came right back with a small glass of milk for Alexis. "This should help, but sip it slowly," he warned, and she gratefully drank it.

"Oh my gosh," she said, when she put down her empty glass. "That was crazy hot!"

Matt shook his head. "Too bad. Looks like you failed the challenge."

"I did not!" Alexis insisted. "I said that I would try it, not that I would like it."

I had to agree. "Yeah, that totally counts. Thanks, Alexis."

Eddie ran to the kitchen again and came back with another plate of food. "I made some nonspicy chicken, just in case," he said, putting it in front of Alexis.

She looked completely relieved. "Thank you so much!"

Now that Alexis's challenge was over, we could all relax and eat our meal. For dessert, Eddie made homemade flan, which is like this sweet, creamy, caramel-y egg custard. It was the perfect cooling end to the spicy meal.

"This is amazingly good," I said. "It might be my favorite dessert ever."

"Better than cupcakes?" Matt teased.

I nodded. "Better. Eddie, you are the dessert master."

Eddie looked really pleased. "Thanks, but I had a dessert the other day that blew me away. It was this really delicate, perfect apple tart with homemade cinnamon ice cream on top. Amazing."

"Oh, you mean the dessert you had at Chez Donald?" Mia's mom asked.

Mia nudged me under the table. I turned and looked at her. That was my father's restaurant! But nobody at the table knew about it except me and Mia. It was weird having such a big secret.

I was dying to talk to Mia about it, but we didn't get a chance until after dinner. Alexis and Emma and Matt had to leave, but it was still early and my mom wasn't picking me up until ten. Mia and I went up to her room to hang out.

"That was so weird, your mom mentioning Chez Donald," I said.

"I know!" Mia agreed. "So, have you talked to your dad yet?"

I frowned. "I'm not sure if I want to. But Mom says he wants to see me."

"It must be hard for you, Katie. But you've got to do what feels right, you know?"

I was quiet for a minute. "I was thinking about your plan," I said quietly.

"You mean going to the restaurant?" Mia asked.

I nodded. "I figured that way, I can get a look at him, and if I feel brave enough, I'll talk to him. But if I chicken out, he'll never know." It seemed like the perfect thing. I could satisfy my curiosity with zero risk.

"Let's do it," Mia decided. "I'll figure out a way for us to get there so no one is suspicious, okay?"

"Thanks," I said gratefully, and I started to feel excited. Soon, I might be seeing my father for what would be the first time in a long time.

CHAPTER 14

Sharing the Secret

I decided I couldn't keep the secret from Alexis and Emma any longer. I waited until we were all together again at lunch on Monday.

"So, I found out a little more about my dad," I said, and Emma and Alexis immediately leaned in, curious.

"Did you e-mail him back?" Alexis asked.

"Did you talk to him on the phone?" Emma wanted to know.

I shook my head. "Not yet. My mom talked to him. She was pretty mad that he tried to contact me without going through her."

Alexis nodded. "I can totally understand that. You said you haven't seen him since you were like, two, right?"

"Right. And Mom said I could see him if I want, but I'm not sure," I explained. "Part of me is kind of mad at him. But the other part of me has a million questions for him, you know? Like, I always wanted to know why he left."

"Didn't your mom tell you?" Emma asked.

"She says he wanted to find himself or something like that," I replied. "But I never understood that. I mean, couldn't he find himself while he was with us?"

Everyone was quiet for a second. It sounded pretty bad for a guy to leave his wife and little kid and just go away. You'd have to have a pretty good reason for that. I really hoped he did.

"Did you find anything more about him?" Alexis asked.

I nodded. "He says he has three kids," I said. "I don't even know if they're boys or girls or how old they are."

"Ooh, if they're boys, then you'll have three brothers, just like me," Emma said, her blue eyes shining.

I smiled. "I thought the same thing."

"And if they're girls, at least they'll be younger than you," Alexis pointed out. "Because big sisters can be a total pain."

"So can little kids," Mia said, and I knew she was thinking of Ethan, who was the son of Mia's dad's girlfriend. I think Ethan is, like, five, and I know he drives Mia crazy.

"Well, maybe I'll never even meet them!" I said, suddenly feeling stressed. "I just don't know!"

"Poor Katie," Emma said. She is a very empathetic person. (I learned that word in English class, and it means someone who can tell what other people are feeling. It's a great word for Emma, because it even has part of her name in it.)

"It's okay," I said. "But I left out the weirdest part. My dad owns a restaurant right over in Stonebrook—Chez Donald."

"Oh my gosh!" Alexis cried. "Mia's mom just mentioned that the other day. My parents go there sometimes. And all this time your dad owns the place. Weird!"

"Totally weird," I agreed. Mia looked at me, and I knew what she was thinking. Did I want to tell Emma and Alexis about our plan? I shook my head. I still wasn't sure if I wanted to go through with it.

That night, I called Mia from my room.

"So, what do you think?" I asked. "When should we go?"

"I'm with Dad this weekend, so we can do it

the next," Mia replied. "I checked their hours, and they're open for lunch. I can ask Dan to drive us. He won't ask any questions. We can tell our moms we're going shopping in town."

That would be a lie, I knew. But wasn't Mom lying to me? And, anyway, it was just a small lie. I wasn't hurting anybody.

"Okay," I said. "In twelve days, Operation Chez Donald is on!"

CHAPTER 15

Chez Freak-Out

The next twelve days were the longest, slowest days of my life. A few interesting things happened. One afternoon, I went to the park again with Mia, George, Ken, Sophie, and Lucy. Another day after school, Emma and I went to the gourmet shop and bought the candied ginger. And on the weekend Mia was with her dad, Alexis, Emma, and I baked two dozen plain-Jane cupcakes for a birthday party (vanilla with vanilla icing), which was a supereasy job. And in English class, Chau wrote a poem about things that go together, and it made me laugh all day, every time I thought about it. It went like this:

Peanut butter and jam,
eggs and ham,

milk and toast,
and potatoes and roast.
These are the things that I like
most.

We had to write a poem for our assignment, and I was still working on mine. Somehow I couldn't quite get it, maybe because my head was in so many other places.

Finally, the day came for Operation Chez Donald. Getting past Mom was pretty easy.

"Mom, Mia and I are going to go shopping," I said.

"Okay. Where?" Mom asked. She was putting on makeup in her mirror—light blue eye shadow! Then she was trying all different things with her hair—putting it up, parting it on the side, fluffing it all out. It was nuts. Who was this new fashion-conscious person in my mom's body?

Anyway, I couldn't completely lie to her. "There's this new boutique or something that opened in Stonebrook, and she wants to go."

If Mom remembered that my dad lived in Stonebrook, it didn't concern her. After all, we go to Stonebrook sometimes. It's no big deal.

"Fine," Mom said. "When are you going?"

"Around eleven thirty," I said. "Dan's driving us."

Mom put down her makeup wand and smiled. "That's nice of him. Your friends have such nice brothers."

"Yeah," I replied, and my heart was pounding. Then I quickly went to my room before she changed her mind.

I was starting to feel more nervous every minute. I had washed my hair that morning, so even though it was still boring and straight, it was shiny and clean. I wanted to wear jeans and a T-shirt, as usual, but Mia checked the restaurant's website, and she said it looked a little fancier than that. So Mia had come over on Friday to help me pick out an outfit from my closet.

I changed into the denim skirt and blue shirt with lace around the collar that Mia had selected. She was bringing me a pair of blue flats with little bows on them to borrow because pretty much all I have are sneakers and beach sandals. When I looked in the mirror, I had to admit that I looked pretty nice.

I wouldn't be embarrassed to have me as a daughter, I thought, and my stomach started to flip-flop. That was one of my worries. What if my father took one look at me and was like, "Uh, no, thanks. I was kind of hoping for someone else"? That would be awful. If everything worked out, he would get to see me in jeans and a T-shirt a lot, but I wanted to make a good first impression.

"My, you look nice," Mom commented as I walked past her room.

"Well, um, Mia said the boutique is kind of fancy, so I wanted to fit in," I said. "No big deal." Then I thought a second. "You know, you've spruced up, so I figured I should spruce up too."

It made sense, right? Even if it sounded a little mean. But Mom didn't seem to notice.

She picked up a tube from her dresser. "Do you want to use some lip gloss?" she asked.

"No, thanks!" I said nervously. A skirt was one thing. Lip gloss was just going too far.

Thankfully, I heard a car beep outside.

"That's Mia. Bye, Mom!" I said, racing to the front door.

"Bye, Katie! Love you!" she called after me.

"Love you too!" I said, and I felt a guilty pang. I really didn't like lying to her like this.

I ran outside and then climbed into the backseat of Dan's car. Mia looked nice, as always, in a black-and-white polka-dot skirt and a white blouse.

"Thanks for taking us, Dan," I said as I buckled my seat belt.

"Whatever," Dan replied. He doesn't talk much, but he really is nice.

Then he took off, blasting heavy metal music so loud that I couldn't talk to Mia at all. A few minutes later he pulled in front of the restaurant on Main Street in Stonebrook.

"We'll text you when we're done," Mia said.

"Okay," Dan replied, and then he drove away.

Mia and I stood outside the restaurant, staring at the sign: CHEZ DONALD.

"I guess this is it," I said.

"It'll be fine," Mia said. "We don't have to do anything besides look at him, remember?"

"But how will I know who he is?" I suddenly realized. "I don't even know what he looks like." I had tried to find a picture on the Internet, but Mom had all these crazy controls, so I could barely get to any pages.

"If he's the owner, then he'll be walking around in a suit and checking on tables," Mia said. "Besides, I think when you see him, you'll just know, you know?"

I nodded. That made sense to me. After all, if he was my father, we probably had some kind of invisible bond, like radar. For a split second I imagined him walking to our table and saying, *Katie! My long-lost daughter!*

"Okay," I said, taking a deep breath. "Let's go in."

We stepped inside a wide, bright space with gleaming, dark wood floors. The walls were pale yellow on top, with dark wood on the bottom half. The tables were set with crisp white tablecloths and gleaming glass.

There was a hostess podium in front of us, and part of me had hoped my dad would be standing there. But instead there was a young woman with sleek black hair pulled back into a bun and red lipstick. She wore a simple, sleeveless black dress.

"May I help you?" she asked us. She looked at us with a questioning look. I guess it was a little weird that two girls like us would be at a fancy place for lunch. I almost wanted to turn back right then and there.

"We'd like a table for two, please," Mia said. She grew up in Manhattan, so she knows how to do stuff like this, which is a good thing, because I was too nervous to say a word.

The hostess looked at us for a minute, then picked up two menus and then led us to a small table in the corner.

111

"Your server will be with you shortly," she said.

"Thank you," Mia said with a sweet smile.

I started nervously glancing around the restaurant. "There're lots of guys in suits walking around! Any one of them could be him," I said in a loud whisper.

"Those are waiters," Mia told me. "They're all dressed alike, see? And they're not wearing suits, just black shirts and ties."

Then a man walked by in a gray suit. "What about him?" I asked.

"He's way too young," she pointed out. "Besides, he's just going to the bathroom."

I craned my neck to look at the tables behind us. "There's a guy in a suit over there."

"And he's eating," Mia said. "Why don't we look at a menu? We're supposed to be eating here, remember?"

"Right. Stick to the plan," I said, picking up the menu. "Oh my gosh! Twenty-four dollars for calves' liver and onion confit? I only brought twenty bucks with me. And what the heck is confit anyway?"

"It's pronounced 'con-fee,'" Mia explained. "Dad and I go to this French restaurant sometimes. Just relax. We can order a salad."

"I don't even see salads in here," I said, frantically

scanning the pages. "What's *'les poissons'*? Poison? Is that some crazy culinary trend?"

"It's French for 'fish,'" Mia explained patiently. "And they do have salads. See? Here." She pointed to a list of salads on the page.

"They're, like, twelve dollars," I said. "For lettuce? That's crazy."

A server came by and asked us if we wanted bottled water. "Tap water will be fine, thank you," Mia replied. Thank goodness for Mia!

"We can each have a salad and some water, and everything will be all right," Mia assured me. "Why don't you just take a deep breath?"

I tried, but it didn't help. My palms were sweating, and I felt shaky all over. "I think I need to go to the bathroom," I said.

I got up and then walked in the direction I had seen that guy in the suit headed. The restrooms were tastefully tucked behind a barrier in the back of the restaurant. The wall leading to the restroom doors was decorated with framed newspaper reviews of the place.

And then I stopped in my tracks.

"Family Man Brings French Cuisine to Stonebrook." That was the headline of this one article. Underneath it was a picture of a smiling guy with brown hair, with his arm around a small blond woman. In front of them were three little girls in frilly dresses. My stomach was tight as I read the caption underneath: "Marc Donald Brown with his wife, Helene, and their three daughters."

Three daughters. No mention of a fourth daughter, Katie Brown, who lives right next door in Maple Grove. I knew I shouldn't, but I couldn't stop reading the article. It was all about how my dad had decided to open his restaurant in Stonebrook instead of New York City, so he wouldn't miss his kids growing up.

"'Family is everything to me,' Donald says. 'I knew what I'd be sacrificing if I were commuting to Manhattan every day. Luckily, I found this space in Stonebrook, just minutes away from home. And I've tried to create a warm, inviting space where families can enjoy coming together.'"

I started to shake. Family is everything? He must have meant his *new* family, because obviously his old family meant nothing to him. Nothing. I started to feel tears sting my eyes. How important could family be to him if he hadn't even seen me or spoken to me since I was two?

Suddenly, I felt Mia's hand on my arm. "Katie, there you are! The waiter came by to take our order, but I told him to wait. Are you okay?"

I was so choked up that I couldn't answer her. Mia followed my eyes to the article on the wall. She was quiet for a minute as she read it, and then I heard her say, "Come on. Let's get out of here."

I didn't argue. I tried as hard as I could to hold back the tears as I followed Mia through the restaurant.

"Sorry, my friend isn't feeling well," she told the hostess as we passed the station, and the woman gave me a sympathetic nod.

Then we were back out in the cool spring air, and my knees almost buckled. It was silly of me to think that lying about this wasn't going to hurt anybody. Because of course it had hurt someone—me.

"I'll text Dan," Mia said. "He shouldn't take too long to get back here."

As Mia texted, I heard the beep of someone activating a car alarm and then looked up. A man was getting out of a fancy black car parked in front of the restaurant. He was tall, with wavy brown hair and green eyes, just like the guy in the newspaper photo.

And then it hit me. It *was* the guy in the photo. I was about to come face-to-face with my dad.

CHAPTER 16

Heartbreak

What happened next felt like it took place in slow motion. Marc Donald Brown walked from his car to the sidewalk. He was swinging his keys and whistling. As he passed me and Mia, he smiled.

"Hello, girls," he said.

Then he kept walking and went into the restaurant.

I froze. My father, my very own father, had just walked right past me. He didn't even recognize me. I started to feel sick to my stomach again.

Mia must have remembered him from the picture too.

"Katie, I'm so sorry," she said.

I didn't answer. I couldn't. Why did I think he would recognize me? The last time he saw me, I was toddling around in diapers. Obviously that invisible father-daughter bond I had imagined was just ridiculous. But that didn't make me feel any better. I thought about the heartfelt reunion I had been dreaming about and felt like a fool.

"I just want my mom," I said. My voice was hoarse.

"Let's wait down on the corner," Mia suggested. "Dan will be here soon."

When Dan picked us up, I didn't mind the heavy metal blasting from the speakers, because it kind of matched what was going on in my brain. The loud music drowned out what I was feeling, and I was glad not to have to talk.

When we got to my house, I ran to the front door. All I wanted to do was fall into my mom's arms and cry. When I got inside, she was in the living room, standing in front of the mirror on our coat closet. She had on lots of makeup and another new dress I had never seen before. This one was really pretty, with blue and yellow flowers.

Suddenly I wasn't sad anymore, I was angry. I knew Mom was dressed up because she was going to see that secret boyfriend of hers. It wasn't fair. I just wanted everything to go back to normal:

just me and Mom, with no dads or boyfriends or anybody else.

"Katie!" Mom said, surprised to see me back so soon. Then she looked at my face, and I could see her worried look creep over her face. "What's wrong?"

I could barely speak. I was shaking. I knew my face was bright pink, like it gets when I'm about to cry. Finally, I just sputtered, "Everything! Everything is wrong!"

I was so angry that I felt like somebody else was in control of my body. I stomped upstairs to my room and slammed the door really hard. Then I flopped down onto my bed. I could feel the hot tears in my eyes, and I just started to cry.

A few minutes later I heard a knock on my door.

"Katie, I've told you that slamming your door is unacceptable," Mom said through the door in her scolding voice. "If you are angry or upset, it's okay, but you need to act your age and try to talk about it. Even if it's just to say, 'I'm in a bad mood and need some time to myself.'"

I lifted my head off my pillow. "Why didn't you tell me you were going on dates?" I yelled. Then I put the pillow over my head. It felt good to get that out.

Mom didn't answer right away. Then I heard the creak of the door opening and felt Mom sit down on the edge of the bed.

"I don't know if they *are* dates, really," she said softly. "I'm just getting to know this person. I enjoy his company. But I didn't think it was appropriate yet to tell you about him, and— Wait a minute. How did you know?"

I took the pillow off my head and then sat up a little. I knew my hair was all messed up and there were tears still running down my face. "You've been different," I told her. "You wear more makeup and you cut your hair. You got all new clothes. You sing. And you've been running with someone in the park."

Mom looked surprised. "Oh! Did you see me in the park?"

"I followed you," I said. I was tired of keeping secrets.

"Katie! I don't like being spied on," Mom said, and for a second she looked really angry. "Sometimes I'm going to do things that don't concern you, and you just need to trust me."

"I know," I said.

"Is there anything else?" Mom asked.

I hesitated for a minute. I wasn't sure if she

would understand about Operation Chez Donald, but I felt like I had to go for it. Like I said, I was tired of keeping secrets.

I took a deep breath. I started to cry again, and Mom stopped looking angry.

"Katie, what else?" she said in a more gentle voice. "What's wrong?"

"Mia and I found out that Dad owns a restaurant in Stonebrook, Chez Donald," I began. "It's . . . it's where Mia's mom and Eddie go a lot. And . . . Well . . . Well, I just wanted to see him, to see how I felt. I wanted to know what he looked like and to see what he would say when he saw me." I stopped. I was crying pretty hard. Mom looked so sad. She put her arm around me and smoothed my hair. I leaned into her arm, and I could feel her take a deep breath.

"Oh, Katie," she said. "What happened?"

And then I told her the whole story about Dan driving us and our plan to just see him and even about the newspaper article.

"Okay, right now I'm not going to talk to you about lying to me, especially about where you are going. We'll talk about that later."

"There's more," I said.

Mom looked at me worriedly.

"He . . ." And I started to cry again just thinking about it. "He . . ."

Then she figured it out. "You saw him?" Mom asked.

I nodded. "But he didn't see me. Well, he did, but he didn't even recognize me, Mom! He drove up to the restaurant and then got out of his car. He looked at me and said hi. Then he walked right by me. He didn't stop. His own daughter! How could he do that?"

Then Mom started to cry.

"Oh, Katie," she said, wrapping her arms around me. Mom cried almost as hard as I did. "Oh, honey, I'm so, so sorry. But maybe he truly didn't recognize you. You look so different now, I can hardly believe it, and I see you every day. The last time your dad saw you, you were still practically a baby. You're a young woman now." She brushed the hair out of my face. "I'm sure your dad would have remembered you if he looked closely."

I let Mom hug me for a while, and it felt nice. After what seemed like a long time, I stopped crying, and we sat there for a while longer.

Finally, she said, "Katie, do you want to meet your father?"

"I don't think so," I replied quickly, and as soon as I said it, I knew I meant it. "Just seeing him today was weird enough. I can't imagine sitting across from him and, like, trying to have a conversation with him, as if everything is normal. Because it's not. I don't understand how he can say family is everything when"—I started to cry again—"when I've never been important to him. I don't understand why he left."

"I don't either," Mom said honestly. "I don't know why he left us."

Then I realized that Mom said "us." I always knew my father left me, but I never really thought about the fact that he left Mom, too. I wondered if she had been as sad as I was knowing that he had another family.

"You never asked him?" I said.

"Like I said before, we haven't spoken in years," Mom said. "You'd have to ask him. All I know is that we were young, and he was nervous about becoming a father. I think he just panicked and left. And then the more time passed, I think, the harder it was to come back to see you. I think he's probably wanted to write that e-mail for a long time, Katie."

I thought that too.

"Here's what I want you to remember," Mom said, holding my face with both hands. "You are very, very important to me. You're the most important thing to me in my whole life. You know that, right?"

I sniffed. "Yes," I said, because I do know how much Mom loves me, but it still felt good to hear. It made me feel stronger. "Right now, I just want things the way I know them, which is just you and me."

Mom smiled. "Well, they might not always just be you and me. At some point I'd like you to meet Jeff. I think you'd like him."

Now that I wasn't angry anymore, I was curious. "What's he like?"

"Well, he's a teacher," Mom said. "And he has a daughter, too, but she's a few years younger than you. And he's a runner. But I guess you knew that, right?"

All these things sounded okay. If he had a daughter a few years younger than me, that wouldn't be too bad. At least she'd be older than Jake or Ethan, and hopefully a lot less whiny and annoying, too. Maybe Jeff would be as cool as Eddie and make spicy food for us.

"Maybe one day I can ask my father about

why he did what he did," I said. "But not now."

"That's fine. I'll e-mail your father back," Mom said. "And I'll let him know that you know how to reach him if and when you're ready. Okay, Katie?"

"Yes!" I replied with a sigh of relief.

Mom stood up. "I'm dressed up, you're dressed up, and I know we're both hungry. Let's go get a late lunch."

"Weren't you going to meet Jeff?" I asked.

"Jeff can wait," Mom said. "Remember what I said? You're the most important thing to me, Peanut Butter. And you always will be. Let me call Jeff to tell him today won't work. Why don't you splash your face with some cool water? Then meet me downstairs in five minutes, okay?"

I nodded. "Just no French food," I joked.

Mom smiled and then went downstairs. I got up to brush my hair and wash my face.

So, one problem was solved. I could deal with my dad later. But it didn't look like this Jeff guy was going away any time soon.

Will he be like guava jelly? I wondered. *Different, but still good? Or what if he's something that isn't good with peanut butter at all, like . . .*

Honestly, I couldn't think of anything that

isn't good with peanut butter. So maybe that was a sign or something. Like everything was going to be okay.

I was just going to have to wait and see.

CHAPTER 17

A Little Spicy, a Little Sweet

The next day I was feeling a lot better about everything. Mom was really worried about me, but just getting it out made me feel a lot better. She kept giving me the worried face all night, but honestly I was good. We had pizza for dinner and Mom brought out all our old pictures from when I was little, just to show me how much I've changed and grown.

After reassuring her about a million times that I was okay and that I'd never, ever go anywhere again without telling her, Mom dropped me off at Alexis's house, so we could make our cupcakes for the PTA dinner. The kitchen there is always sparkling clean and perfectly ordered, with nothing on the counters to clutter things up.

We quickly got to work on the batter.

"So, what's the plan tomorrow night?" I asked. "We just need to drop these off, right?"

"I was thinking that we could stay and pass out cupcakes," Alexis said. "That way, if someone says they like our cupcakes, we can give them a business card in person."

"Are we allowed to do that?" Emma asked.

Alexis nodded. "I've already e-mailed the president of the PTA, and she said okay. We won't be served the dinner, though, so we'll have to eat beforehand."

Mia nodded. "That sounds like a good idea. Our parents are going, anyway, and we can do homework after school."

"So, what did you guys do yesterday?" Emma asked.

Mia and I looked at each other. I decided I might as well tell everybody.

"We went to my dad's restaurant to check it out," I said. "It's fancy and expensive. And I saw my dad for, like, a second, but he didn't recognize me."

Emma and Alexis froze. Then Emma's face melted. "Oh, Katie, that must have been awful!"

"I had a big freak-out. And then when I got home, my mom told me that she has a sort of boyfriend. His name is Jeff."

"I knew it!" Alexis said. "Did she tell you anything about him?"

"Just that he's a teacher, and he likes to run, and he has a daughter who's younger than me," I said. "Oh, and I forgot to tell you. It turns out my dad has *three* daughters."

"Didn't you always want a sister?" Mia asked. "If your mom stays with Jeff, and you end up seeing your father, you'll have, like, four of them!"

I couldn't even imagine that. "Aaaah! I can't think about that right now. For all I know, Mom will break up with Jeff and I'll never get together with my father. Then things will just be the same. Right now I don't want to see my father. But it looks like Jeff might be sticking around. That's all I know."

Everyone took a minute to take this in. Then we all started talking about other things as we finished the cupcakes. After we filled and iced them, Emma brought out the little bag of candied ginger we had bought.

"They *do* look like little jewels," Mia said.

"What do they taste like?" Alexis asked.

"A little spicy, and a little sweet," I said.

Alexis reached into the bag. "Are you sure you want to do that?" I asked her. "I thought you didn't like spicy."

Alexis shrugged. "Nothing can be as spicy as Eddie's green-chile chicken. And I'm curious."

She took one of the smaller pieces and popped it into her mouth. Then she smiled.

"This is really good," she said. "Sure, it's spicy, but the sweetness balances it out. Our cupcakes are going to be awesome."

"I'm so proud of you!" Emma teased.

Alexis kind of got me thinking. Maybe things were going to stay the same with me and Mom, but deep inside I knew that probably wasn't true. So I'd have to be brave, like Alexis, and give things a try. If I was lucky, there might be some sweetness to balance things out.

"We are going to be a huge hit tomorrow night," I predicted. "I just know it!"

On Monday night, we got into our best business mode. We have these Cupcake Club T-shirts that Mia made for us, and we made sure to wear them. Alexis printed out a fresh new batch of business cards, and she had printed out a sign for our table: CUPCAKES BAKED BY THE CUPCAKE CLUB, STUDENTS AT PARK STREET MIDDLE SCHOOL.

The PTA dinner was held in a banquet hall in town, one of those fancy-looking ones with Roman columns along the walls and fake plants in big brass urns everywhere. The tables were decorated in blue and yellow, the official colors of Park Street Middle School.

We set up our cupcake table while the PTA parents ate salad and pasta and chicken. We have these nice-looking tiers with big round platters on each level, and we use them a lot to display our cupcakes. The PTA had ordered ten dozen cupcakes, so there were a lot to set up. But it looked really nice when we were finished.

It was kind of boring waiting for the PTA to finish eating, and a couple of moms got up and gave long speeches. Emma's mom had brought us sandwiches to eat, so we finished them and waited quietly. But things picked up when it was time to get the cupcakes. The parents crowded around the table, and we couldn't give them out fast enough.

Everyone took the cupcakes back to their tables, so they could have coffee and talk some more. Nobody asked for a card.

Alexis frowned. "Maybe we didn't need to come tonight after all."

But then something really cool happened. As people finished their cupcakes, they started to come up to the table.

"That was one of the most unique cupcakes I've ever had," one woman said. "What kind of jelly was inside?"

"Guava," Alexis replied, handing her a business card. "We are available for parties, meetings, or any occasion, and we can customize your cupcakes to your taste."

I love Alexis. She is a born saleswoman.

The woman looked impressed. "I will certainly keep you girls in mind. Can I have a few more cards for my friends, please?"

Alexis happily handed over the cards.

"See?" Emma said. "You were right, Alexis. It's good that we came."

A man and woman came over. "Which one of you is Katie?" asked the man.

"That's me!" I said.

"It's so nice to meet you, Katie. We're Mr. and Mrs. Martinez!" he said. "George's parents. He talks about you all the time."

"He does?" I asked.

Mrs. Martinez smiled. "He's mentioned your cupcake club. He's right, you make delicious cupcakes,"

"Thanks!" I said. "And tell George I said hi!" As soon as I said it, it felt weird. Why would I tell his parents that I said hi if I was just going to see him the next day? Ugh. Weirdness.

Then a blond-haired woman approached us. "Mrs. Delfino told me I should talk to you girls. You organize children's parties, right? My twins are turning four, and I need to invite all twenty kids in their preschool class, but I have no idea what to do!"

Alexis, Emma, and Mia all looked at me.

"What do you think, Katie?" Mia asked. "Are we still doing children's parties?"

For a second, the face of a screaming five-year-old flashed through my mind, and I shuddered. It would have been easy to say "No way!" But I knew that doing new things was they way to go.

"Sure," I said. "We'd love to organize your party for you."

The woman looked completely relieved. Alexis handed her a business card. "E-mail me with the details, and we can discuss some options for the party," she said.

"Katie, what gives?" Mia asked, when the woman walked away. "I thought you had enough of screaming kids."

I shrugged. "I don't know. I just decided that sometimes change can be good. Like guava jelly instead of grape. You can keep the tried and true, but not be afraid of something different once in a while. Sometimes, you have to try a new recipe, I guess!"

My friends all grinned. "Like something spicy!" said Alexis.

"Or something scary," volunteered Emma.

"Or something that totally doesn't feel like you!" Mia chimed in.

"Exactly!" I said.

For some reason Chau's funny poems popped into my head, and I thought of how mine would sound:

> Grape and guava, too.
> Tried and true.
> And a little new.
> Good friends do
> stick together like glue.

It wasn't perfect. It needed a few changes. But it was getting there.

Want another sweet cupcake?
Here's a sneak peek
of the fourteenth book in the

CUPCAKE 🧁 DIARIES

series:

Mia
a matter
of taste

The Worst News Ever

"Okay, Mia, open wide."

"Open wide" might be two of the scariest words in the English language, don't you think? Because when you hear them, it usually means a dentist is about to look into your mouth.

Not that I have anything against dentists. My dentist is Dr. Brown, though I normally call her Mrs. Brown since she is my friend Katie's mom. She's supernice, and I'm sure most dentists are perfectly nice people. I just don't like the stuff they have to do.

Anyway, the person asking me to open wide wasn't even Mrs. Brown. It's her assistant, Joanne, who is also really nice. She's tall, and she wears her blond hair up in a ponytail all the time, and under her blue scrubs I can always tell that her clothes are very fashionable.

Joanne must have noticed the nervous look on my face.

"It's cool, Mia. I'm just taking some X-rays. This doesn't hurt at all. You know that, right?" she asked.

I nodded. "Okay."

I opened wide, and Joanne stuck this white square thing into my mouth and told me to bite down. Then she straightened the heavy gray apron covering me and left the room. I heard a quick buzz, and then Joanne came back in and took out the square thing.

"You know, this really isn't that flattering," I joked, looking down at the apron.

She laughed. "Just a few more shots and you can take it off, and then you'll be ready for the runway again, okay?"

Joanne was right—the X-rays didn't hurt at all, but I was glad when they were over.

"Dr. Brown will be by in a minute to go over them with you," Joanne told me. "I'll send in your mom, okay?"

"Thanks," I said, and inside I felt a little bit relieved. Up until a couple of years ago, I lived in Manhattan. Mom and Dad worked during the day, and my babysitter always took me to the dentist. Now we live in the suburbs, and Mom mostly works from home and has her own company, so she has more time to do stuff like this. It's nice having her around, especially at the dentist's.

"How'd it go?" Mom asked as she came into the room.

"My teeth are superclean," I said, flashing her a smile. "And Joanne said it doesn't look like I have any cavities. So I'm thinking I deserve some kind of reward for being so awesome."

Mom raised an eyebrow. "You want a reward for not getting any cavities?"

"I was thinking a trip to the mall would be good," I said.

"Well, you don't have to twist my arm for that," Mom replied. I guess it's a good thing we both love shopping!

Then Mrs. Brown came in, wearing a white dentist coat. She has the same friendly brown eyes as my friend Katie, but Mrs. Brown's light brown hair is cut short, with long bangs that are stylishly angled across her face.

"It looks like you're cavity free, Mia, but let me take a look in person, okay?"

I nodded and opened my mouth again.

"Very good," she said with a nod. Then she looked at me and then at my mom. "But we should talk about your X-rays."

She pressed some keys on the computer on the table next to me, and these pictures of my mouth popped up. It was really weird to see how long the roots were underneath my gums, and I turned my head away. My teeth looked too creepy!

"Mia's got some crooked teeth on her bottom jaw, and her top jaw as well," Mrs. Brown said, pointing to the screen with the end of her pen. "Her bite is misaligned, which can cause problems down the road. I'm recommending you see an orthodontist. I'm not sure, but Mia may need braces."

A cold chill went right through me.

"Braces? Seriously?" I asked. It sounded more like I was squeaking, because I was so upset.

"Well, as I said, I'm not one hundred percent sure," Mrs. Brown said. "But it's very likely."

I looked up at my mom. I could already feel my eyes starting to well up with tears. I started shaking my head. "No way! I cannot get braces. I will die!"

"Mia, it's okay," Mom assured, putting her hand on my shoulder.

Mrs. Brown gave me a sympathetic look. "I understand. Nobody wants to hear news like this.

But by correcting your teeth now, we can help make sure your mouth stays healthy for a long, long time. I have some brochures I'll give you, so you can find out what it's all about."

Then she turned to my mom. "I know a great orthodontist over in River Glen. I'll get you her card." She smiled at me. "She's the same doctor Katie used when she had her braces."

Mrs. Brown left, and I looked at Mom. "Please tell me this isn't happening!"

"There's no need to panic yet, Mia," Mom said. "Let's wait and see what the orthodontist says before we start worrying, okay? And anyway, braces aren't so bad. Katie had them! And your cousin Marcela had them, remember?"

Marcela is a junior in high school now, but she had braces when she was my age. I definitely remembered them. How could I forget a mouth full of metal and wires? I shuddered.

"She was always complaining that they hurt," I pointed out. "And when we all went to that farm she couldn't eat a candy apple, and she cried."

"That's just what you remember. I know that most of the time, she was fine," Mom said, and then she quickly changed the subject. "Hey, we should get out of here and get to the mall!"

Mom's strategy worked—at first. I never get tired of going to the mall. Since my dentist appointment was right after school, I was kind of hungry, so Mom got me a vanilla mango smoothie at Smoothie Paradise. I sipped the delicious tropical goodness through a straw as we slowly walked around, window shopping.

"Well, if I get braces, at least I can still have smoothies," I remarked, and Mom smiled.

"That sounds more like my Mia. Stay positive!"

But I ruined my own mood by bringing up the braces, and it didn't even help when we went inside Icon, my favorite shop in the whole mall. They had all the new summer styles on the racks, in tons of bright, almost fluorescent colors.

I held up a neon-yellow sleeveless dress. "Wow, you could wear this in the dark and people could see you for miles," I said. I actually look good in yellow, so I brought the dress to the mirror and held it up to my face.

I posed and smiled, and then suddenly I got a vision of myself in the bright yellow dress with a mouth full of blinding silver metal.

"There is no way I can wear this if I get braces!" I wailed. "It's too much! Aliens in space will be able to see me."

"Oh, Mia, that's not true," Mom said, trying to reassure me, but it was no use.

"If I get stupid braces, I won't be able to wear any of the new summer styles!" I complained. "I might as well go live under a rock somewhere!"

Mom sighed. "Come on, let's go to the candle shop. I think you need some calming scents."

I could feel tears stinging my eyes as I followed Mom out of Icon. And the scent of misty mountain sandalwood candles (my favorite) did not help one bit. I was convinced that braces were going to ruin my life!

🌸 Cupcake Girls Haiku 🌸

A haiku is a type of poem. It only has three lines, but there is one important rule you must follow. The first line has five syllables, the second line has seven, and the third has five. Read the haiku poems below about the girls in the Cupcake Diaries books. Then you'll have a chance to write some of your own.

 ### Katie

Smart, cute, and funny.
She started the Cupcake Club.
Her friend George likes her.

Mia

Fashion is her thing.
She turns heads in the hallway.
Always looks her best.

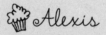 ### Alexis

Fiery red hair.
She loves to figure things out.
Has a crush on Matt!

Emma

She's a girly girl.
She's so pretty—a model!
Loves her Cupcake friends.

Your Turn!

Here's your chance to try writing your own haiku poems.
Write one about your favorite Cupcake girl here:
(If you don't want to write in your book, make a copy of this page.)

....
(NAME)

_____

_____

_____

Now write one about yourself or your best friend!

....
(NAME)

_____

_____

_____

A Little Sweet Talk

There are 11 words in the puzzle. Can you find them all?
Circle every word you find. Then write the leftover letters, in
order, on the lines below. You will find out something that
happens in the next Cupcake Diaries book, *Mia a Matter of
Taste*.

(If you don't want to write in your book, make a copy of this page.)

Word List:

ACTIVITIES, BAKE, BALLOON, ICING, NUTRITION, PARTY,

RAINBOW, SHOELACES, SPRINKLES, TROPICAL, UNUSUAL

```
A  C  T  I  V  I  T  I  E  S
S  E  L  K  N  I  R  P  S  G
I  C  I  N  G  Y  T  R  A  P
E  N  U  T  R  I  T  I  O  N
T  L  A  U  S  U  N  U  S  E
R  A  I  N  B  O  W  B  R  K
N  O  O  L  L  A  B  A  C  A
E  T  R  O  P  I  C  A  L  B
S  E  C  A  L  E  O  H  S  S
```

Now write the leftover letters, in order on the lines below to find out
something that happens in the next Cupcake Diaries book.

In *Mia a Matter of Taste*, Mia _ _ _ _ _ _ _ _ _ _ _ .

In *Mia a Matter of Taste*, Mia **GETS BRACES.**

Answer Key

Coco Simon always dreamed of opening a cupcake bakery but was afraid she would eat all of the profits. When she's not daydreaming about cupcakes, Coco edits children's books and has written close to one hundred books for children, tweens, and young adults, which is a lot less than the number of cupcakes she's eaten. Cupcake Diaries is the first time Coco has mixed her love of cupcakes with writing.

Want more

CUPCAKE DIARIES?

Visit **CupcakeDiariesBooks.com**
for the series trailer, excerpts, activities,
and everything you need for throwing
your own cupcake party!

Simon
Spotlight

Still Hungry?
There's always room for another Cupcake!

Katie and the Cupcake Cure
978-1-4424-2275-9 $5.99
978-1-4424-2276-6 (eBook)

Mia in the Mix
978-1-4424-2277-3 $5.99
978-1-4424-2278-0 (eBook)

Emma on Thin Icing
978-1-4424-2279-7 $5.99
978-1-4424-2280-3 (eBook)

Alexis and the Perfect Recipe
978-1-4424-2901-7 $5.99
978-1-4424-2902-4 (eBook)

Katie, Batter Up!
978-1-4424-4611-3 $5.99
978-1-4424-4612-0 (eBook)

Mia's Baker's Dozen
978-1-4424-4613-7 $5.99
978-1-4424-4614-4 (eBook)

Emma All Stirred Up!
978-1-4424-5078-3 $5.99
978-1-4424-5079-0 (eBook)

Alexis Cool as a Cupcake
978-1-4424-5080-6 $5.99
978-1-4424-5081-3 (eBook)

Katie and the Cupcake War
978-1-4424-5373-9 $5.99
978-1-4424-5374-6 (eBook)

Mia's Boiling Point
978-1-4424-5396-8 $5.99
978-1-4424-5397-5 (eBook)

Emma, Smile and Say "Cupcake!"
978-1-4424-5398-2 $5.99
978-1-4424-5400-2 (eBook)

Alexis Gets Frosted
978-1-4424-6867-2 $5.99
978-1-4424-6868-9 (eBook)

Katie's New Recipe
978-1-4424-7168-9 $5.99
978-1-4424-7169-6 (eBook)

Mia a Matter of Taste
978-1-4424-7435-2 $5.99
978-1-4424-7436-9 (eBook)

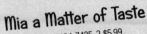

If you liked

CUPCAKE  DIARIES

be sure to check out these

other series from

Simon Spotlight